MW01487777

TAKE A HIKE

MIMI GRACE

Copyright © 2023 by Mimi Grace

Print ISBN: 978-1-7389062-0-8

Cover design and illustration by Leni Kauffman

Editor: Lopt & Cropt Editing

Proofreader: Johanie Martinez-Cools

All rights reserved.

No part of this book may be reproduced without written permission from the author, except for the use of brief quotations in book reviews.

This is a work of fiction. Names, characters, places, and incidents either are the product of the author's imagination or are used fictitiously, and any resemblance to actual persons, living or dead, business establishments, events, or locales is entirely coincidental.

CONTENT NOTES

These brief notes are for readers who need some insight into the contents of this novel. Some may view the following as spoilers.

- Deceased friend (dies before the start of the book)
- Brief recollection of an accident and recovery
- Sexually explicit scenes

Chapter One

THE DECISION-MAKING part of the human brain is said not to fully develop until a person is twenty-five years old. This may explain why Raven Coleman, at nineteen, bought a one-way ticket to Paris to follow a guy she'd just met and fallen for at a music festival.

The relationship was a bust, as one can expect of something built on a foundation of booze and vibes. However, she still left the City of Love with pictures that needed cropping but were suitable for her social media feed. She also had the memories of visiting crowded landmarks, eating butter-laden pastries, and being entertained by bronze living statues who, despite provocation from tourists, did not break their poses.

It was those painted street performers Raven currently imitated, almost eight years later, as she stood stock-still holding a tray of hors d'oeuvres.

"Gruyère and crab palmiers," Raven said to the guests reaching for the offerings.

It was a perfect summer evening for a garden party, but

it was undercut by a general strangeness. As if everything was computer generated.

A jazz band played lively music, but people weren't dancing. It was also unlikely that anyone would get drunk or laugh louder than the clink of their cocktail glasses. And when she told a lady, "Oh my God, I love your earrings," she apparently disrupted a simulation that required she be as charming as an insentient hologram. Her tendency to chat and flirt would not be rewarded here.

Once her tray was bare enough to warrant a refill, Raven crossed the lawn, passing a water fountain to a set of stone steps that led her into a galley kitchen bustling with the people responsible for making the party run smoothly.

Distinct voices were lost in the chaos, but the chef's cut through. "If I ask for something sautéed, why in God's name would you give it to me fried?"

Raven took a minute to massage a knot in her shoulder and confirm with other servers that the partygoer in burgundy shorts was indeed a creep. After a swig of water, she was ready with a fresh tray of food to serve.

Tail ends of conversations and harsh perfume followed her about the garden, and when summoned by a guest with a glance, she quickened her steps to deliver. "Grilled oysters with lime and ginger," she would tell them, and she repeated this routine until another blip in the simulation changed the course of the evening.

A man tripped.

Perhaps on a raised stone or the toe of his fancy loafer. Regardless, the result was the same: The man reeled forward with his eyes bugged out and hands searching for leverage. To save the tray and herself from going down, Raven swung her body sharply out of reach. But in doing so, she transferred all that momentum to an unsuspecting woman, bumping her right into the basin of the water fountain.

Chatter and music came to an off-key halt as everyone turned to gape at the lady splashing in the shallow water.

Raven knew her fate even before the woman screamed and pointed at her.

"Off with her head!" the shrill noise seemed to demand, and minutes later, she was standing in front of her boss.

"I've got to let you go for today," he said.

He looked sorry about it too. Not likely for her sake, rather, being one waitress down would disrupt the flow of service.

As she was quickly ushered to gather her belongings, she mouthed, "It's okay, it's fine," to the other servers, who looked on as if she were actually being led to a guillotine. And maybe she'd feel that way too if her weekly horoscope hadn't forewarned a shake-up in her working relationships.

A stone-faced security guard was the final checkpoint before Raven could exit the mansion, and while he searched her purse with the finesse of a burrowing mole, she said, "I'd have taken the Chardonnay, but the bottles wouldn't fit in there."

The man slowly raised his head, pinning his eyes on Raven.

"Oh, not that face," she said, laughing nervously. "I was kidding."

Eventually, she was permitted to leave the home and trek to the front gate. Having arrived as a passenger in a carpool, Raven was left to text the most reliable person on her phone to pick her up.

By the time she got to the end of the driveway, four meteorological seasons later, her best friend, Gwen, was waiting.

"Why do rich people like phallic-shaped hedges so much?" her friend asked once Raven entered the car. She was studying the oblong greenery surrounding them.

"There's a psychosexual explanation, for sure," Raven said. "But I want to go my entire life not knowing those details."

"So what happened?" Gwen asked as she got them out of the ritzy neighborhood. "I thought this gig was supposed to end much later."

"I got fired."

"No, stop. Ray," Gwen said, briefly averting her eyes from the road to Raven.

She was a schoolteacher by trade, so straitlaced on principle. Getting fired was unimaginable to her.

"Why?" Gwen asked.

"I made out with the band's saxophonist and told the host her party decor was wack," Raven deadpanned.

"See, that scenario is plausible, so I have no idea if you're fucking with me."

Raven coyly smiled but detailed the truth, and afterward, her friend asked, "Does this mess with your apartment-hunting plans?"

"No, the rental market is what's messing with my plans. And if I'd known it was this bad, I might've worked it out with the other guy."

Up until a few months ago, she'd lived in a one-bedroom apartment with a view, but with an impending rent increase, Raven had told her landlord, in so many words, to kiss her ass. She'd thought she'd find better. In reality, everything was similarly expensive and competitive, so she'd been forced to temporarily move back in with her mother.

"Come to the movies with Tony and me tonight. Get your mind off things," Gwen said.

"Tempting, but it's okay, girl," Raven said, removing the hair tie that held her long braids in a bun.

The many hours she'd worked that week were starting to settle across her body. Plus, while Gwen wouldn't mind her tagging along, Raven couldn't imagine her friend's boyfriend would be happy with her crashing date night.

"I'm gonna get home, eat whatever least healthy snack my mom has in the pantry, and call it a day," Raven said.

Tomorrow had to be better, certainly.

A tune, one of the standards the jazz band played at the party the night before, was stuck in Raven's head. She sat cross-legged on her yoga mat with her eyes closed, trying desperately to quiet her mind long enough to meditate. But the silly little notes persisted for a while.

When her brain finally released them, she was promptly seized by thoughts of the bedroom she currently occupied. How small it was. How most of her earthly possessions sat in boxes surrounding her. It didn't take long to feel like the walls were closing in, and at that point, she gave up on her morning ritual altogether.

She threw on her robe and followed the whine of the blender downstairs to the kitchen where her mother, in a short slip dress and flexi-rods in her hair, was blitzing a smoothie.

Raven and her mom were two peas in a pod. They'd been getting confused for sisters since Raven was a teen. They were both air signs, tall, and lovers of accessories.

The only immediately obvious difference between them was their body types. Where her mom was slender from a steadfast Pilates regime, Raven had a fuller figure that made wearing the short skirts she preferred an extreme sport.

"Tell me what you think," her mother said, handing her a glass of grayish-green sludge.

Raven took a tentative sip. "Earthy."

She traded the drink for an apple and headed to the breakfast nook, scooping up her mother's cat from the hardwood floor.

"Morning, GoGo," she whispered, peppering the feline's neck with kisses.

"I didn't expect to find you home when I got in last night," her mother said, joining her at the table with her smoothie and a store-bought loaf cake to share.

"Got fired over some bullshit."

"That's annoying. I'm sorry," her mother said.

"At least I don't have to wear that scratchy uniform again."

"Always you with the bright side," her mom said with some humor.

"How was your evening? How's Bob?" Raven asked while cutting into the cake and plopping a slice on each of their plates.

"Calvin," her mother corrected.

"Calvin, sorry."

For as long as Raven had been dating, she and her mom called every guy they were seeing but weren't serious about Bob. If the men turned out to be worth a damn, they'd graduate to being referred to by their actual names in conversation.

"He's great. And I'm great because his divorce was finalized yesterday."

"Fucking finally," Raven said, playfully poking her mom's leg with her foot. "I was starting to worry."

"We might've celebrated a little too hard last night, though. Poor guy is upstairs with a hangover."

"Happy for you," Raven said. It made her heart full to see her mom glowing and in love; she deserved it after all the frogs she'd kissed.

"Are you really okay, angel?" her mom asked gently.

"Yeah, I'm fine. A little antsy. Unsettled."

"Why's that?"

"I feel like everything is happening in grayscale," Raven said. "I think I need to go on a retreat or something where I can't touch my phone or access the internet. Gain clarity and reconnect with my intuition."

It took losing her apartment for Raven to realize she'd been going through the motions. She valued flexibility and freedom, and she'd sculpted her life in a way that allowed her to embrace that. But that lifestyle was in contention with how she'd been raised.

As an only child of a single parent, she'd learned to save for rainy days, practice frugality, and budget for everything. So once the riotous chapter of her early twenties ended, she felt the need to seek financial security. She took a secretarial position with benefits at her friend's middle school and worked side jobs to build up her savings and pay off debt.

But what now? She was unclear about what she wanted to do in the next chapter of her life.

"There's this desert retreat I've been looking at," Raven said. "But you don't want to know the price."

"Why don't you call your astrologist lady instead?" her mom asked.

"Because Ida's booked till the fall."

"It'll be okay," her mother said. "You'll land on your feet. You always do."

Raven knocked the wooden table to stave off bad luck. "Let's hope."

"Oh, shit. It's already nine," her mom said, standing. "We need to get going soon."

"We? Where?" Raven asked, reaching for another slice of loaf cake as her mother picked up the plate to store it.

"Remember that meeting with the lawyer."

Raven had forgotten all about that. Her grandfather (in DNA only) had died earlier that year. His aversion to work and a decades-long love of blackjack made any worthwhile inheritance doubtful. So the Coleman women showed up at the lawyer's office, wedged between a KFC and laundromat, not expecting much.

A paralegal led them into a room made of dusty surfaces and teetering stacks of paper.

The lawyer, Mr. McGowan, a man in his late sixties with a distractingly wrinkled dress shirt, entered minutes later.

"Natalia Wash?" Mr. McGowan asked after shuffling through files on his desk.

"No, Patricia and Raven Coleman."

He chanted their names while thumbing through his unorganized pile before pulling out a certain folder. "Here you are."

"So what did the deadbeat leave us?" her mom asked.

The lawyer, confused, responded, "Deadbeat?"

"I know, I know. He looked the part, but I promise you my father was no family man," her mom said.

"Ma'am," the lawyer said, coughing uncomfortably, "I'm the estate executor for Charles Hulme, not your father."

"Charles?" her mom said, her hands shooting up to cradle her face. "Chuck is gone?"

"Three months ago, in a hiking accident," the lawyer explained to them.

"Oh, God," her mom said with a small laugh and welling eyes. "I knew it would be those damn woods that would take him."

"I'm so sorry," Raven whispered, dabbing the tears that fell down her mother's face. She assumed the man was a coworker at the nursing home because she couldn't immediately place the name.

But then her mom said, "You remember Chuck, don't you? I dated him for a few years when you were in middle school," and a memory surfaced.

"He got me that iPod Nano for Christmas that one year," Raven said reflectively.

Her mom had dated an older white guy with long hair and a mustache whose jeans had always looked dirty. Raven remembered him being kind and having a funny laugh.

The lawyer excused himself from the room to find his misplaced reading glasses, giving Raven a chance to ask her mother, "Why would he leave you anything? It's been so long."

"I know he put us both in his will while we were dating, so he must've forgotten to change it after we broke up."

"There's probably someone out there pissed about that," Raven said.

Mr. McGowan returned with glasses on his face, and he proceeded to explain the limits of the will and his role as the executor. Then came the reading of the Last Will and Testament of Charles Hulme.

"This part is for specific bequests," the lawyer began. "I leave Patricia Coleman, if they shall survive me, for their own use absolutely, the following: storage unit full of collectibles."

Apparently, Chuck had a unit located a couple of hours outside the city full of vintage weapons he'd amassed. Donation and a garage sale were the only recourse for Raven's mother, who admitted, "I hate those things. I have no use for them."

"And I leave to Ray Coleman," the lawyer continued, "if they shall survive me, for their own use absolutely, the following: Mountaintop Adventures Company, located in the municipal district of Cedar Lake."

Raven shifted forward in her seat, unsure she'd heard correctly. "Wait, he left me a company? Like, a currently operating one?"

"Yes, an outdoor recreation and tour service."

"Okay, wow," Raven said as she looked at her mom, who appeared similarly stunned. "What am I supposed to do with that? I don't want to run some random business."

Again, Mr. McGowan shuffled through his papers and produced a coffee-ring-stained document. "There's a buyer, a Silas Reynolds. He has shown deep interest in purchasing."

Raven scanned the Offer to Purchase. It presented the terms of the sale, disclosed business debts, legal obligations, and finally, a price. The amount of money being offered made Raven's head spin, and she reached for the citrine crystal on her necklace as she reread everything.

The figure had more zeros than she'd ever seen at once in her bank account. It was several expensive-desert-retreats type money. A down-payment-on-a-modest-home type money.

"What are you thinking?" her mom asked her.

Raven laughed, then picked up a pen. "Tell me where to sign."

"That will have to be done in person or through another lawyer you hire," Mr. McGowan said.

Not interested in wasting any time, Raven said, "Then I guess I'm heading to Cedar Lake."

Chapter Two

THE DRIVE to Cedar Lake was a journey through the prairies to the Rockies. Trees and mountains jutted high from the earth, a sight worthy of the poems they'd inspired.

All Raven knew about the small town, however, was that it produced a portion of the country's lumber and didn't have a reputation for fun like Whistler or Banff.

As she neared her destination, hotels of varied sizes and ratings started to appear on either side of the small freeway. Not long after she passed the town's welcome sign, she arrived at the motel she'd booked mainly for its low price point. Inside the small reception area, she found a woman with silver hair thrown roughly into a ponytail, poring over a crossword puzzle.

"A nine-letter word for an ancient symbol of wholeness or completion," the lady said without looking up.

With no one but the two of them in the lobby, Raven assumed the older woman was asking for help, so she said, "Infinity?"

"Tried it already. Only has eight letters."

Raven dropped her bags, approached the desk, and studied the crossword for a minute.

"Oh, what's that image of a snake eating its tail called?" Raven asked, tapping her temple to help the word emerge. "It starts with an *o*."

She'd seen it once on a tarot box.

The lady, Linda—as she later introduced herself— stared off into the distance for a while before her face grew wide with a smile, and she scribbled down the letters that made up the word "ouroboros."

"Thank you," Linda said, grinning. "And welcome to Cedar Lake."

Once Raven had been checked in, she left the office for her room with extra pillows and complimentary cookies. She found a clean space and a massive bed, so sleep came easily.

In the morning, with GPS as her guide, she left the motel and drove through the town's still-quiet main street until she hit a narrow road that took her up a mountain. Pine trees stood on either side, forming a canopy above where only some sunlight managed to peek through the gaps in the branches and needles.

"Where the hell..." She pressed close to the steering wheel, trying to spot civilization.

Before she could worry, a sign appeared: "Mountaintop Adventures, 8 Kilometers Ahead." And minutes later, after turning onto an unpaved path, a cabin in a grass field bracketed by an imposing forest materialized.

Raven approached the cabin and parked her car next to a shuttle bus and four pickup trucks differing only in color. The butterflies went into full effect when she cut the engine; she was still wrapping her head around the idea of coming into a lot of money.

As she made her way to the steps of the main office,

the confident stride she'd intended had a tipsy-off-mimosas wobble to it because of the gravel under her heels. So when Raven reached the entrance, she took a few seconds to recenter.

"Embrace it. Claim it," she said, touching the citrine pendant on her necklace.

When she opened the door, however, the mayhem within stopped her cold.

Three people, a middle-aged blonde woman wielding a broom and two younger men, were running around the disarrayed cabin.

They were chasing something. A squirrel, Raven quickly realized.

"Close the door!" the woman shouted, and Raven scrambled inside, slamming the door behind her and making herself as small as possible against a wall.

The tiny rodent continued to evade capture, leaving his pursuers breathless in its wake.

"Bodie! Get to the other side! We'll corner him there," the woman said, and the jacked white guy among them darted to follow instructions.

Once in position, Bodie turned to the lanky man wearing a band T-shirt and asked, "Where did you put the nuts?"

The only response was a Ziploc bag traversing the air in an arch from the band T-shirt guy's hand to Bodie's, who dumped the nuts into a small pile on the floor.

The squirrel, now calmer, was coaxed by the woman and her broom toward the food. It eventually took the bait.

What now? Raven thought just before a thickset man with skin the color of rich coffee grounds entered the room carrying a blanket.

He stood tall and sturdy like the mountain they were on but moved with the poise of an ice skater as he leaped over a table and overturned chairs to reach the cornered squirrel.

"Careful now, people," the man said, his voice low and singsongy as he inched closer to the squirrel.

Raven braced for another chase, but the man gently swept the rodent into the blanket folds, eliminating that possibility.

"Oh, thank God," one said as the group surrounded the cradled squirrel.

"Did he break the splint?"

"Yeah, we gotta redo it."

Raven stood there for a few minutes, watching them coo over the animal. She was unsure they remembered she was there, so she politely cleared her throat.

"Hi, sorry to interrupt," Raven said when four heads turned in her direction.

The big man with dark skin handed off the squirrel and stepped forward to meet her with a striking smile. He had a full beard that she thought functioned well as a frame to hail others to take notice of his perfect smile and teeth. "Welcome to Mountaintop Adventures. What can I do for you, ma'am?"

His voice was robust and complex. It filled the space his body didn't and reminded Raven of the aural bliss of a sound bath meditation.

"I'm looking for Silas Reynolds," she said, pushing all other thoughts aside for business.

"That's me," the man before her said.

"Great," she replied. "I'm Raven. The new owner."

Silas Reynolds had loved blueberries ever since he was a child. But he'd found that blueberry-flavored snacks never accurately captured the essence of the fruit. So his brain always needed a moment to accept the gap between what he knew blueberries tasted like and the medicinal extract food companies used.

That was the type of experience he was currently having looking at the woman in front of him.

Raven.

The new owner?

He'd been expecting the beneficiary of Mountaintop today, yes, but he assumed it was someone around Chuck's age, maybe a buddy from his time in the army.

This woman was none of that. She looked like she'd run through a Party City store with all the colors and sparkle that made up her outfit.

There had to be some mistake.

"Sorry, you're Ray Coleman?" he asked.

She laughed lightly like he'd told a joke. "Yes, I'm Ray —Raven Coleman."

"And Chuck left this place to you?" Halo, the bluntest among the Mountaintop team, asked.

"He did," Raven said as she pulled a document from her purse and presented it to Silas.

It was Chuck's will. The group crowded around him to look at the papers that had become almost mythical to them. For months, Silas had been in contact with Chuck's lawyer, Mr. McGowan, trying to understand the succession of the business. This mysterious will had been cited as the reason he could not own Mountaintop Adventures.

But it still begged the question, why did his former boss leave the business to someone no one had ever heard of?

"How did you know Chuck?" Silas asked the woman.

"He and my mom dated when I was young," she replied. "But he must've forgotten to take me off his will when their relationship ended."

Silas nodded. It was an understandable oversight, and since they'd be sorting it out momentarily, there was no harm.

"Let's get this paperwork over and done with then, shall we?" he said, and as he led her out of the central area of the cabin, he received encouraging thumbs-up from the others.

In the break room, Silas retrieved a file from the top shelf in the kitchen cabinet before turning to face Raven. She was assessing the space, and he took a moment to do the same with her.

He noted details he'd easily missed when taking her in all at once. Everything about her popped, not just her clothes. It was also the shiny lipstick on her lips, her long red nails, and the dark hue of her skin.

She was also tall. Very tall. She didn't need to so much as tilt her head upward to meet his eye. The heels she wore definitely helped, but it was still a feat not many people in this town could manage.

"Thanks for coming all this way," he said.

"Of course," she replied. "Also, this place has a really cool aura."

Silas took a sweeping look around the worn kitchen they used as a break room, office, and occasional first aid station. "The bad lighting is doing a lot of work."

"No, I mean, there's good energy in here."

Silas didn't know how to respond to that, so he just said, "Thanks," and gestured for her to take a seat.

"You're an outdoorsy tourism business, correct?"

"Yeah, we provide outdoor experiences from basic survival skill classes to forest-walking tours, and as of last year, we offer hotel pickups in our shuttle."

"And what do you do or teach?" she asked.

"I'm the archery instructor."

"Oh, very cool," she said.

For several minutes, Raven casually flipped through the Offer to Purchase documents Silas had given her, and he tempered his impatience and desire to hurry her along by occupying himself with his phone.

"This keeps you busy?" Raven asked, finally breaking the silence. "Like, do you have enough business to sustain yourselves?"

"Summer is our peak, but we operate year-round. And we've been going for fifteen years, so something's working."

"Would it be weird for me to ask how much you earn?"

Silas stilled. "Personally? Yeah, a little."

"Forget it then," she said with a wave of her hand.

What was with all the questions? Was she trying to get him to pay more for this place? He'd made a fair offer that had been corroborated in an official business valuation. It was also the offer he'd made Chuck, and the older man would've accepted it too, if it hadn't been for his untimely passing.

"Everything okay?" he asked as she continued to study the contract.

"I've never really owned anything," she said. "The most expensive thing I have is my car. And I still have eight months of payments left on it."

Silas straightened, now on full alert.

"I might like owning a place like this. I don't know," she said with a shrug, and a gust of air that escaped him morphed into a hearty laugh. She could not be serious.

"Why are you laughing?" she asked.

"You can't do that," he said bluntly.

"Why not?"

"You have no idea how to run this business."

"I'm a fast learner, and I have a lot of experience that I think will be helpful."

The humor of the situation evaporated all at once. "No."

"No?" she asked, her sculpted brows rising high.

Admittedly, it was not the best thing to say at the moment.

"Ma'am, just sign the papers," he said as measuredly as possible. "You'll get your money, then you can pay off your Toyota Camry or whatever."

"No," she said, echoing his earlier tone.

The situation was quickly turning sour. This woman could not be what lies between him and his goal of owning the business.

"I'm open to negotiating the price," he said, preparing himself for an absurd counteroffer.

"What you're offering seems fair to me," she said.

It made no sense then. Maybe she thought owning the business would be an easy stream of passive income.

"This isn't some hands-off job, okay?" Silas said. "Being the boss means being responsible for expenses. Dealing with town ordinances. It means making sure that everyone out there has a check to take back to their families. Keeping Chuck's legacy alive."

With every responsibility he added, he saw the assuredness in her face slip a little more.

Good.

He needed her to smell the pine forest and wake the hell up.

"Okay, I hear you," she said. "And I'm not committing to selling or staying. I'm only asking for some time to weigh my options and make an informed decision."

Silas rubbed his neck roughly, trying not to get frustrated with a dead man for all this confusion. "How much time do you need?"

"Let's say... the summer."

"The summer?" he bellowed, almost tipping himself backward off the chair. "You want to take the whole summer to make a decision?"

"Yeah, I can spend it observing and learning how things work around here. Get a sense if this is a business I want to run."

"You don't have a life somewhere else? A job to get back to?" he asked.

"No, actually. My schedule's free until September."

He blinked as his mind raced in search of a solution, but his efforts proved futile. There was no convincing someone this impulsive of anything right now.

"All right, you'll stay the summer," he said.

"Perfect," she said, rising to her feet. "I'll see you tomorrow, and I hope we can work well together."

Silas ignored the part of him that wanted to roll his eyes in response to her words and offered a simple nod of acknowledgment instead.

"Also, do you have any places you'd recommend I get breakfast?" she asked as he walked her to the front.

"Try the Yodeling Loon," he said flatly.

After she left the cabin, Silas turned to see the Mountaintop team pop up from behind the reception desk with a sheet cake and big smiles. As they opened their mouths to sing or shout something, Silas cut them off by saying, "She didn't sign the papers."

"What?" Halo asked, casting a look at the door Raven had left through. "Is she coming back?"

"Yup, tomorrow," Silas said, moving to straighten a chair that had been upturned. "And the next. And the next. For the entire summer."

He explained what had gone down, their faces falling before settling into expressions Silas thought likely reflected his own.

"Chuck wanted you to own this place. Literally everyone in town knows that," Doc, the baby of the group, said. His youthful face belied the fact that he was the smartest person Silas knew.

"Not according to his Last Will and Testament," Silas said.

"This is bullshit," Halo said. "What can we do?"

"Absolutely nothing. We'll have to wait till the end of summer to see what she wants to do."

"God," Halo said, rolling her eyes. "A woman like that, in a town like this? She'll get bored in a month."

"More like a week," Silas said, but he wasn't so sure that was true; he'd seen the stubborn glint in Raven's eye. But he was trying to assure them all would work itself out. They didn't need to worry.

"You want to make that an official bet, dude?" Halo asked, lifting a brow.

A petty bet as a bluff of confidence couldn't hurt, so he said, "Drinks on me at Blue's for a month if she doesn't bail by the end of this week."

He and Halo sealed the agreement with a handshake.

Bodie, the resident survival expert at Mountaintop, had been quiet all this time but now asked with genuine seriousness, "So we're not eating the cake today?"

There was technically nothing to hurrah about, but Silas said, "No, let's eat it. It'll be an early celebration."

———

An exhilarating fizzy rush swept over Raven as she left the Mountaintop Adventure's office.

She owned a tour company.

The excitement of that reality clung to her as she drove down the mountain straight to the diner Silas had recommended. It was time for celebratory pancakes.

The Yodeling Loon was a cozy restaurant with a giant loon sculpture at the front and waitstaff in matching aprons. It smelled like cinnamon buns, and the people inside looked like some version of patrons she'd seen before. There was the table of old men talking loudly to one another behind their newspapers, the folks inhaling their breakfasts before they needed to clock in, and dozing workers who'd just ended their shifts.

Once inside a booth, Raven placed her order with a waitress then looked out the window at the store façades on the other side of the street. She could picture the glittering snow that would appear come wintertime. If all worked out, she'd be here to see it.

Raven's phone buzzed with an incoming call from Gwen. It was as though her heedful best friend sensed, all those miles away, that pragmatism was being evaded.

"How'd the meeting go?" Gwen asked.

"It was fine," Raven began. "Unexpected."

"Unexpected? Wait, explain."

"I had the bill of sale right in front of me, and all I kept thinking about were the odds of me getting fired the day before I learned about an inheritance. Or the odds of a boyfriend my mom dated almost fifteen years ago forgetting to remove me from his will. It all feels synchronous."

The opportunity also surfaced just as Raven had begun to feel the pull of ennui. It was a sign, and Raven paid attention to signs. From the obvious ones that told her how to comport herself on the road to the subtle ones the universe sent her way to take that job, dump that boyfriend, or buy a dress on sale.

"So you're just going to own a tour company?" her friend asked. "You're the least outdoorsy person I know."

"No, I'm doing a trial run and will make a final decision at the end of the summer."

An old version of Raven would've been all in by now, so her current plan felt judicious. There was virtually no risk to it.

"And the would-be buyer is okay with this?" Gwen asked.

"That would be a no," Raven said, laughing.

She'd been a little sad to see Silas's charming smile shift into a scowl. But she supposed she couldn't blame him for being irritated by her change of heart. Nevertheless, she wouldn't be persuaded to do what he wanted. In fact, the way her personality was set up, she didn't do well at all with people telling her what to do.

"All right. What about the practicalities?" Gwen asked. "Did you bring enough clothes for the summer?"

"No, but I'll call my mom to send a suitcase on one of the long-distance buses that passes through."

"Okay, where will you live?" her friend then lobbed. "I'm assuming you're going to pay yourself a salary while you're there, but hotels still aren't cheap."

"I'm staying at a motel right now, and I'll talk to the owner and work out a deal or something," Raven said.

Gwen sighed heavily. "I guess this will be another one of your adventures."

"Yes, exactly," Raven said, smiling at her friend's familiar refrain.

Everything would work out fine. She could feel it. Nothing as small as logistics or a territorial man would be insurmountable.

Chapter Three

THERE WERE 2,156 posts on Raven's Instagram.

Silas had been trying to learn about the woman who now owned Mountaintop but somehow got sucked into a wormhole of her social media feed that kept going and going. Selfies. Quotes. Group photos. Travel pictures. More quotes. Antique clocks and furniture. An orange cat who he learned across several posts was named Van Gogh and belonged to her mother.

Spellbound by the photos in front of him, Silas startled at the sound of his doorbell. It had grown dark without him noticing, and he switched on the lights as he walked from his kitchen to the front door.

As he neared, he could hear his niece and nephew, five-year-old twins, talking on the other side of the door.

"Who goes there?" he called out with an exaggerated low voice.

"Maggie and Leon," they replied together.

"I know no one by those names. I'll need the secret password."

The twins burst into giggles, but Maggie, the diplomat of the duo, said, "Uncle Silas, it's us!"

Silas cracked the door open so only his head could fit through. He ignored his brother to look down at his niece and nephew and study them as if they were faraway stars.

"Oh, of course! Maggie and Leon," he said, widening the door.

The twins raced past him, and he followed them to the kitchen, where they waited in a specific spot. Silas lifted them both into his arms, and they opened a cupboard stocked with their favorite snacks.

"One each," their father instructed from behind.

"I think two would be okay," Silas whispered to them.

And once they had their chosen snacks, they left, chatting unintelligibly, for the living room.

"You spoil them," his older brother, Isaiah, said to him.

"It's my purpose on this earth," Silas replied.

Separated by three years, the Reynolds brothers looked similar enough, but Silas always said his brother was the sophisticated one.

"Where do you keep your corkscrew? I brought champagne to celebrate." Isaiah said, rummaging through his drawers. "Well, actually, it's sparkling cider because, you know, weeknight."

"It's in the far left one, but there isn't anything to celebrate at this very moment," Silas said.

"The ink still drying?" Isaiah asked.

"No, ink not used."

This bit of information made his brother abandon all bottle-opening efforts. "What happened?"

"Raven Coleman happened."

"Am I supposed to know who that is?"

"She's the one Chuck accidentally left the business to. She's taking the summer to decide whether to stay or sell."

"Damn. So you're under new management until further notice?"

"Yup. And if that's not bad enough, she has zero clue about the tourism industry," Silas said. "But if I can help it, she'll run Mountaintop in name only until she makes her final decision."

He had to mitigate the damage she could potentially inflict on the business.

"I can get Victor to look over the will and see if there's any leeway," Isaiah said.

"Yeah, I'd appreciate that, man," Silas said.

His brother's husband had been some big shot lawyer before he left it all behind to be a novelist and partner to a small-town veterinarian. It couldn't hurt to hear his thoughts.

"What's this?" Isaiah asked, picking up a brochure from the cluttered breakfast table. "You thinking about getting your competition coaching certification?"

"Nah, it's part of the random junk mail I get sent every month," Silas said, snatching the brochure from his brother before he could see the margin notes and highlights.

"You could do it, you know? Your portfolio is impressive," Isaiah said. "And it would get you out of Cedar."

"Sounds like you're trying to chase me out of town," Silas said.

"No, of course not, but I know you're not the biggest fan of change, so I'm just reminding you that you don't have to be chained here because it's where you currently happen to be."

His brother's words nagged at something tucked away in his soul, but Silas ignored it to wryly reply, "Your faith in this washed-up athlete is beautiful, truly."

"It's *my* purpose on this earth," his brother said with too much sincerity.

"Also, screw you. I got a lot going on," Silas said as he motioned around them at the kitchen in mid-renovation.

This whole home was a reno project that he was slowly working through. This summer, he planned to tackle a shelf installation in the living room and finish the bathroom and the yard.

"I like the paint choice on the cabinets. Hate the hardware," his brother said to which Silas rolled his eyes. "Okay, where did you say that bottle opener was? We're going to cheers to good luck instead."

"I can't believe you got the stain out," Linda said as she inspected the motel lobby carpet Raven had scrubbed and vacuumed.

"I'm telling you, hydrogen peroxide with some dish soap is key," Raven said.

She'd been up for two hours, cleaning the reception office, setting up the continental breakfast area, and helping Linda with her daily crossword. It was part of the agreement Raven had entered into with Linda for a discounted price on a room with a kitchenette for the summer.

The older lady had been wary of the deal at first, but once she'd discovered Raven was the mystery benefactor of Mountaintop the town had been speculating about for months, she'd changed her tune. Whether it was because she wanted to help a future neighbor or be close to a source of gossip, Raven wasn't sure.

Her commute to work was picturesque, and she got to the cabin before anyone else. For a few minutes, she was able to listen to the birds and set an intention. When Silas arrived, pulling up next to her car, it was without the smile he'd easily given her yesterday.

"You're early," he said as he hauled a duffle bag from the back seat of his truck.

Mere observation or admonishment?

"First days are for good impressions," she said, aware the heels and skirt she wore made her look unserious.

When they entered the cabin, she silently trailed behind him, noting every task he completed on her phone. From the order he turned on the lights to where he placed his personal belongings.

"What are you doing?" he asked, stopping in the middle of drawing the blinds on the windows.

"Taking notes," she replied.

"Why? Of what?"

"I told you I wanted to know how things are run around here, so I'm observing."

He opened his mouth but then closed it before returning to the chore at hand.

Eventually, the two of them entered the break room, where Silas pulled a mug out from a cupboard and said, "You can stop surveilling me now. I'm only making coffee."

Raven put her phone away, knowing she was about to experience the most gnawing silence of her life. And as they stood on opposite sides of the kitchen, him thumbing through the mail as his coffee brewed and her pretending like the laminate countertops deserved closer assessment, she wondered if her entire tenure at Mountaintop would be like this.

"What if I doubled my offer?" he asked as she began to adapt to the idea of never hearing a human voice again.

"I'm sorry?" she asked.

"What if I doubled my offer for the place?"

"Why? Are you?"

"No, only wondering," he said.

"If you bid twice the market value, I'd take the money then call you a fool."

His lips lifted slightly, and after fifteen minutes of straight brooding, Raven was happy about the variation.

As opening hours drew near, the rest of the staff began arriving one by one.

First was Doc, an Indigenous guy who wore a T-shirt of a band she didn't recognize and had a habit of running his hand through his shaggy hair every so often. She learned he did the walking tours for Mountaintop and was getting a degree in plant biology at one of the universities in the province.

"I'm assuming you're the reason for the Chinese evergreen at the front."

"You know plants?" he asked, his face brightening.

"Not officially or anything. Just an aspiring plant mom," Raven said.

The next to arrive was Bodie, a survival expert who could apparently start a fire in under thirty seconds and, if his massive traps and arms were any clue, liked to lift.

"This is Chestnut," Bodie said, lifting a small crate holding the squirrel with a bandaged foot she'd seen yesterday.

"Hi, Chestnut," Raven said, waving to the rodent.

"Oh, he doesn't speak English yet. I'm still teaching him," Bodie said, and Raven laughed but quickly realized from the resolute position of Bodie's brows and mouth he was very serious.

Halo was the last of the team to show up, and her heavy footsteps made her presence known the moment she walked into the cabin. Unlike everyone who had been at least polite, Halo did not attempt to hide her annoyance at seeing Raven.

Their introduction, in which Raven learned Halo was a skilled and nationally recognized rock climber, had barely any breathing room before the older woman launched into questions.

"What are your intentions with this place?" Halo asked, her arms crossed tightly.

"I'm not here to mess with your guys' flow," Raven responded. "I just wanna help."

"And also to potentially, permanently own Mountain-top," Halo countered.

"Well, yeah—"

"Are you good with business?" Halo asked. "Got some degree from a fancy school, maybe?"

"No, but—"

"Any outdoor skills? Hunting or fishing? Been camping before?"

"I once waited in line for thirteen hours to win Coachella tickets at a radio station. It felt kinda like camping."

Her joke got a tiny laugh from Doc, but that was it.

The barrage of questions ended when Halo stalked away to pour herself a cup of coffee, and Raven was paid no further mind until it was time to start the workday.

As they all filed out of the kitchen, Raven quickened her steps to catch up to Silas before he could disappear.

"I was thinking I could observe everyone today," she said to him. "Maybe I can join whoever does the morning shuttle pickups."

"Yeah, that won't work," he said.

"Why not?" she asked as they stopped walking to speak more directly.

"Because…"

"Because what?"

He was scrambling for what to say and blinking far too much.

"Because I have something more important you can do," he finally said, leading her across the cabin to a supply room that looked like the inside of Mary Poppins's carpet bag. That was to say, it was a glorified junk drawer.

"We've been meaning to clear this out for years," he told her.

Raven leaned forward from the safety of the threshold to get a better look at the cramped space haphazardly stuffed with miscellaneous items she couldn't even identify.

"And this is urgent?" she asked.

"Relatively," he said.

She was unsure if he thought her naïve or passive enough to go along with what was clearly bullshit.

Everything in her wanted to call it out. She hated being dismissed, but she wasn't trying to execute a hostile takeover. If she had to do some obvious busywork to prove she was serious and committed, she would.

"Consider it done," she said.

When Silas left, she took a few minutes to devise a plan, change into a pair of flat shoes she always kept in her car, and drown out her surroundings with earphones and a playlist. First thing she tackled was the confused mess on the floor. She came across banquet tables and chairs, a dry-erase board on wheels, a wooden sign that read "Mountaintop Adventures: The Rockies Await!", a lawn mower, and boxes filled with tapes and DVDs of different *Rambo* movies. If she couldn't carry something out of the closet, she dragged it.

When she set about unpacking the overstuffed shelves, she was forced to do it slowly and carefully for fear everything would collapse. Despite all her care, she still managed to smash her fingers between the lid of a toolbox. Her only solace as she cradled her hand against her chest was that none of her acrylic nails had broken.

Time passed, but Raven didn't realize how much until Silas reappeared in the doorway.

"We're having lunch if you're interested," he said, giving the room a cursory look but providing no commentary.

He left as abruptly as he'd appeared, missing Raven's mocking smile.

With grime and dust coating her hands and clothes, the restroom was her first stop, but she found Halo blocking her path in the hallway.

The older woman didn't notice Raven at first, too absorbed with the hushed but sharp conversation she was having on the phone. "No, Libby. Yeah, because I said so, that's why. How's that?"

The muffled voice on the other end shouted something, to which Halo responded, "Don't you dare hang up on—"

She'd been hung up on. And it was while Halo was pocketing her phone that she and Raven made eye contact.

"Sorry, I wasn't eavesdropping," Raven said quickly, pointing to the restroom door she'd been trying to reach, and Halo responded by wordlessly stomping past.

When Raven joined the others in the break room, the conversation and laughter trailed off as she was noticed. But with her head held high, Raven retrieved her lunch and took the empty spot next to Bodie.

"How was everyone's morning?" Raven asked and was met with a weak chorus of "Fines" and "Goods," and for a while, muted chewing and Chestnut's squeaking were the only sounds filling the room.

She hated being the reason for the stilted energy, so she thought hard for something to generate conversation.

"What's up with all the *Rambo* on VHS in the storage closet?"

The question got everyone looking up from their food and prompting some laughter.

"Those were Chuck's," Doc explained with a small smile. "When our Blockbuster shut down, he bought every last *Rambo* DVD and tape they had."

"What was he like? Chuck. I ask because I only knew him from a child's perspective," she said. Before she could worry if her question was too sensitive, Bodie—the guy with the massive traps—grinned and said, "A legend. He faced a bear and lived to tell the tale."

"Wait, an *actual* bear?" she asked.

"Yup," Bodie said, his chest puffed out like it was his accomplishment.

"He was bigger than life," Halo said wistfully from her place at the other end of the table.

"And that laugh," Silas added, launching into an impression that sounded like a chain-smoking Santa Claus.

Then everyone took turns attempting their version of the clearly beloved man's laugh.

Raven smiled even when the conversation ceased to involve her and moved on to other topics. The fact they weren't silently eating anymore felt like a victory.

Once lunch was over, the group headed outdoors again, and Raven was left to continue decluttering.

She filled the kitchen sink with soapy water and set to cleaning the dirt on the newly emptied shelves. Amid this work, sometime later, a commotion in the cabin slipped past her earphones during the quiet part of a song.

Initially, Raven thought Chestnut the squirrel was on the loose again, but she left the storage room and followed the raised voices to the kitchen and found Silas and Halo with mops and towels, sopping up a very wet floor.

"What happened?" Raven asked, horrified at the scene.

Silas straightened from his stooped position and pinned her with heated eyes. "You left the tap running."

It was an absurd accusation—she knew how to work a tap.

"How?" she asked.

"The faucet doesn't stay closed on its own," he said, pointing to a little plastic contraption she'd totally removed when filling up the sink earlier. "We keep it in place with that."

"I-I didn't know."

"Okay, now you do," Halo said. "So don't just stand there, help!"

And she did, the air thick with what Raven assumed was their wish for her to spontaneously combust.

Chapter Four

ON DAY TWO OF PURGATORY, Silas arrived at Mountaintop with a plan. One that would see Raven preoccupied for the rest of the week.

Yesterday he'd managed to forget she was even around. She'd been too busy cleaning and organizing the storage room to meddle or be anyone's shadow. It had been perfect, of course, until the Great Flood.

"I'm sorry about yesterday," she said to the entire team when she arrived, presenting them with store-bought cookies.

This seemed to satisfy Bodie and Doc, who dug into the baked goods, but Halo didn't relax her frown.

It really wasn't Raven's fault. She couldn't have known about their DIY plumbing fix, but Silas had done enough absolution and couldn't stand doing any more. If Raven had just signed the papers and gotten out of town two days ago, the whole mess would've been avoided.

"I made you a list," Silas said to her once all the morning pleasantries had been spoken. "It's the different things that need to get done around the cabin."

"So, chores," she said.

"Tasks, chores, whatever you want to call them," he said, handing her a scrap of paper with words he'd scribbled down while eating breakfast earlier that morning.

"Finish organizing the storage room," she read aloud. "Answer customer service emails. Dust surfaces inside cabin. And clean interior and exterior of shuttle van... I can do that."

Each task was deceptively simple; she'd have no time to lurk or pry.

And as Silas predicted, he didn't see Raven all day except during lunchtime, where she showcased the two nails she'd broken finishing up the storage room.

"This one," she said, lifting her left pinky with a now-jagged nail, "hurts like a bitch."

Raven spent the next day answering customer service emails. A straightforward endeavor, sure. However, Mountaintop's inbox had been neglected for months, and the boxy desktop they used in the office was so old it took thirty seconds to load each page.

Throughout the day, he'd enter the cabin to greet his waiting students and find Raven frustrated.

"Come on, come on. Don't freeze on me again, baby," she said on one of those occasions, hitting the side of the wheezing computer.

It took her a full day and a half to complete that job.

Afterward, she started tackling the dust in the main area, which made everyone feel like they'd been transported to the stampede grounds after the horses and cattle had kicked up the dirt. Windows and doors had to be propped open. But the fresh air didn't curb Raven's incessant sneezing.

"Sorry," she shouted into the cabin when a particular

loud sneeze drew attention. "I promise I'm not sick. It's the dust."

For her troubles, however, the cabin was left with a gleam Silas had not been aware was possible.

The following day at lunch, Raven entered the break room sporting scraped elbows and wet jeans. She'd been cleaning the shuttle and had only narrowly won a battle with a tangled water hose.

It was on this day, while Raven was applying Neosporin to her wounds, that Halo sidled up to Silas as he microwaved his food and whispered, "I think I might owe you a drink at the end of the week."

Silas didn't dare hope, but if his plan to keep Raven occupied drove her out of town, he'd fucking take it.

When the last workday rolled around, Raven didn't look like the person Silas had met at the beginning of the week. Gone were the heels, the styled hair, and any attempts at superfluous conversation. She now sported a number of mosquito bites and sighed between sips of her coffee in the morning like she was trying to muster up energy for the work ahead.

Silas squashed any sympathy that arose for her. This would literally be her life as an owner. If she was unable to handle it, the exit was clearly labeled.

———

"You're almost there," Gwen told Raven over video call. "A little to your left."

"I swear I'm going to dislocate my shoulder," Raven said. She was in her motel room, straining to apply ointment to a bite on her back. But it was all worth it when the medicine made contact and relieved the itch.

She didn't know what she'd thought owning a business

would feel or look like, but it wasn't this. In addition to the bite on her back, there were her mosquito-bitten arms, annihilated nails, a mysterious rash on her collarbone, and a scraped knee beginning to scab.

In contrast, her friend lounged on her living room couch with a bowl of cherries in her lap, her deep skin tone beautifully darkened from a day spent in the sun.

"Besides sustaining injuries, how are things?" Gwen asked as Raven climbed onto her bed to relieve her sore quads.

"Fine, maybe? I don't know. I start every morning by cleaning the front reception of the motel," Raven said. "Then I go to Mountaintop to do tasks that somehow require the competency of a juggling, unicycle-riding rocket scientist. There's no Starbucks in sight, and their Timmies never has what I want, so I haven't had good coffee in a week. And for as small as Cedar Lake is, I should've seen a little bit more of the town by now. But all I do is work and come back to this room to recover from the day."

"Raven," Gwen began gently, "I say this with all the love. Maybe this tourist company thing isn't for you. Like I've never heard you complain this much."

Raven shook her head at first, mostly on instinct. She was used to fighting for a lot of things—respect, relationships, money. This had to be growing pains.

"I like some things about this place too," Raven said. "It looks like a *National Geographic* cover with all the trees and mountains. I've met some nice people. There's Linda, Bodie, and even Doc—and sidenote, I found out yesterday that's his nickname because he used to wear knock-off Doc Martens as a teen. And—"

"Okay, I love the quaint small-town trivia, but, girl, you're miserable."

Raven shut her eyes as if that might shield her from the truth. "I thought I was stronger. I've worked retail during the holiday season, for God's sake."

"Come back. Come back to me, Raven," Gwen said in a haunting timbre of a ghost or a sage witch.

"I think the first thing I'd do is get a massage," Raven said, leaning back on her headboard.

"Yes! And I'd meet you there with a grande caramel macchiato with oat milk and extra foam."

"Oh, then we'd go to the flea market," Raven said.

It was her idea of a perfect weekend day, and visualizing it had her feeling happier than she had in several days.

"You know what, you're right. Fuck this place," Raven said as she got up and retrieved the bill of sale that had made a home under her makeup bag all week. "I'm not quitting. I'm just letting go of what no longer serves me."

As she searched the room for a pen, she continued spouting her spontaneous manifesto, speaking about peace of mind and not having to prove anything to anybody. When she returned to the bed, it was in time to see her friend's boyfriend enter the apartment in the background of the video call.

"Your man's home," Raven said, watching Anthony approach the couch to hug Gwen from behind. The camera on her friend's end canted to a weird angle.

"Hey, hey. Still here," Raven said, snapping her fingers when the murmurings and kisses went on too long. The camera straightened to focus on her friend's face once again. Her eyes were glassy, and her lipstick had shifted.

"All right, I'm back," Gwen said with a dopey smile.

"We can pick this up later if you want," Raven said playfully.

"No, I'm here for you," her friend said, rearranging herself in her seat.

"You've already helped, babe. Go have fun."

Her friend hesitated but ultimately said, "Okay, love you. Text me if you need anything."

"Love you too, and hi, Tony."

The camera swerved to her friend's boyfriend, whose usual serious expression appeared for a few seconds before the screen went black.

Now alone in her room, Raven studied the deed. She'd given working at Mountaintop her best try. It wasn't for her. And with that acceptance, an immediate peace filled her. She'd get her money and return to the city with more options than she'd ever had.

The next morning, when she arrived at the cabin for her final day, she found Bodie, Doc, and Halo talking in the break room.

"Have you guys seen Silas?" she asked during a pause in their conversation.

"In the shed, I think," Doc replied, and Raven decided to wait for him in the kitchen and mark the end of her time at Mountaintop with one last cup of mediocre coffee.

It somehow tasted better than it ever had.

"You look chipper today," Halo said with no real curiosity. It was simply something to say.

Over the week, the older woman's attitude had changed from outwardly hostile to bored regard. And God, it felt good to know that today would also be the last time Raven had to deal with it.

"I'm leaving," Raven told them. "Today's my last day."

The soft buzz of fluorescent lights above was the only sound left as everyone grew still and fell silent.

"You signed the papers?" Halo asked tentatively.

"Yeah, I just need Silas's signature, then it's all his."

Raven expected some expression of glee from the older woman—a clap, a cheer, a "good riddance"—but it was Bodie who broke into a grin and said, "Oh, shit. Halo, that means you lost."

Doc elbowed Bodie's side, and the smile on the buff man's face dropped as his lips clamped together.

Raven, confused, asked, "What does that mean? Lost what?"

No one answered her at first, but Raven let the silence stretch as she surveyed the three of them. The men averted their eyes. Halo did not.

"We had a little wager going, that's all," the older woman said.

"A wager?" Raven asked, her heartbeat taking up a quickened rhythm. "On what?"

"It was all in good fun," Halo said, her nonchalance dimming as she seemed to notice Raven's unease.

"Okay, but what was it about?" Raven asked again.

After moments where Halo must've been contemplating what to say, she replied, "How soon you'd leave."

"And who won?" Raven asked, but she didn't need an answer this time because she knew. She fucking knew. And it pissed her off that a bunch of strangers had assessed her and decided what she was and was not capable of.

Silas chose that moment to walk in. The air was tense, but he didn't feel it and gave a casual "How's it going?"

His self-assuredness tipped Raven over the edge, and without hesitating, she retrieved the signed bill of sale from her bag and ripped it in half.

"I'm great," she said. "Excited for the day."

Chapter Five

WHENEVER SILAS WAS over at his brother's home, he expected to contend with a couple of things. Like, at least one of the five family dogs would use him as a resting post. Today, the four-year-old pit bull rescue, Ollie, was lying across his feet under the dining table.

Also, one could bank on Isaiah and his husband, Victor, going off on a tangent to argue the ins and outs of a book or movie Silas had never heard of.

"His home was literally a panopticon, a clear representation of the prison his lifestyle had become," Isaiah said authoritatively.

"I simply don't agree," Victor scoffed.

Silas's niece, Maggie, took advantage of her fathers' momentary distraction to transfer all the peas on her dinner plate to Silas's. And Silas, her unrepentant coconspirator, gobbled them up.

"Papa, Daddy, I'm done," she said, presenting her empty plate.

"Me too," Leon parroted despite still shoveling food into his mouth.

"Okay, thirty minutes of TV, then it's teeth, then bed," Isaiah said, and the kids got up and rushed to the living room.

Before the husbands could enter another debate, Silas said, "We good to talk about the will now?"

It was all he could think about the entire day, and he wanted relief from the mental burden. He needed some good news. The type that sounded verbatim like, "The will is invalid, and you're free to run the business as you see fit."

"Right, yes," Victor said, rising. "Let me get it."

In the meantime, Silas helped his brother clear the table.

"You want some strawberries and whipped cream?" Isaiah asked in the kitchen. "Please say yes. The garden's been bearing a lot this season, and neither of us has had time to do any canning."

"Have I ever said no to dessert?" Silas asked.

They returned to the dining room with bowls and found Victor already seated with the papers.

"Well?" Silas asked his brother-in-law as he settled back into his chair.

Victor began by removing his thin glasses, a bad sign.

"I looked over the will, and unfortunately, I don't see anything that would make me question its legitimacy."

Silas felt like a balloon that had popped. His shoulders slumped, and a distressed grunt left his lips. "I can't do anything about it? Nothing at all? I'm not above doing something slightly illegal."

"I'm going to pretend you didn't say that. Legally, I don't see on what grounds you could contest the will."

"Fuck," Silas said.

Balance had almost been restored. Mountaintop had essentially been his yesterday; Raven had signed the bill. But within seconds, all had been rescinded because of a small bet and a bruised ego. There was no explanation, no apology Raven was willing to hear after that.

"I just changed my mind," she'd calmly stated when he'd approached her with the torn contract. She couldn't even admit that her discovery of the bet had facilitated said change.

"Being patient is all you're left to do," Isaiah said.

"You sound so much like Pops," Silas said, exasperated.

Their father had a collection of proverbs he liked to dole out, regardless of whether they were trite or presently helpful.

"If she's as miserable working at Mountaintop as you described, then you shouldn't worry too much," Victor said. "A person can't do something out of spite forever."

"Oh, that's so not true," Isaiah said to his husband. "The Waynes and the Bardots can't stand each other. And that's been going on for generations."

"Okay, so according to your brother, you're doomed," Victor said.

"No, there's still a lot of hope," Isaiah said. "All I'm saying is you have to hang in there and not let her presence get under your skin."

It was the only way forward.

With nothing more to say on the subject, Victor pulled out a sleek binder he'd been toting around for weeks and said, "All right, let's talk about the party. There's a little less than a month until the twins' birthday. Silas, are you still good to make the party favor bags?"

"Yeah, man. Whenever the materials arrive, send them my way," Silas said.

He wasn't an arts and crafts guy, but he'd offered his help with the planning process. Granted, that was before he found out they were throwing a big circus-themed party, complete with a bouncy castle they were renting from out of town, food catering, and a performance by someone Victor would only refer to as the "special guest."

Silas had made the mistake of teasing Victor about the grand plans, missing his brother's signals to abort the jokes.

"This is the first birthday where their hippocampus is developed enough to form long-term memories," Victor had said indignantly. "I'm going to throw them a party worth remembering."

Silas never questioned any of the party choices again.

"Also, I meant to ask you if you mind us inviting Desiree," Victor said.

Silas frowned. "Why would I care?"

Desiree had been the twins' babysitter when they were toddlers. She was now a product manager at the sawmill.

"Because you two dated for a while," Victor said.

"We went on one date over a year ago."

"Now, why did I think it was more serious than that?" Victor asked, looking over to his husband, who shrugged.

"I have no idea, but you're free to invite her," Silas said.

"Anyone you'd like us to add as a plus-one, then?" his brother asked.

"Are you asking if I'm seeing someone right now?"

"Yes, I thought my question was thinly veiled enough to make that clear."

"No, it'll just be me and a ton of presents for Leon and Maggie," Silas said.

Dating in a small town was weird. Silas had known practically everyone around his age since birth. Those in town who were destined to be together had made that official years ago. The remaining ones, like him and Desiree, would try, at some point, to create a romantic spark, only to find out that familiarity and friendship had deadened the possibility.

Half the reason his brother had been so excited to leave for college in a major city was, as a gay Black man, he could finally have an active dating life. Ironically, it was back in this very town he'd ended up meeting the love of his life.

Silas eventually wanted to find love too, but he was in no rush. Besides, at the moment, he had more pressing issues to attend to.

———

"Okay, ready?" Raven called from inside her motel bathroom.

"Ready," came the voices in the main room.

She walked out, hands on her hips, to reveal her outfit.

Linda, who'd come to Raven's door to deliver fresh towels, had been lured into staying by the fun of the one-woman fashion show underway. She sat on the bed holding a phone with Raven's mother on the screen.

"Thoughts?" Raven asked, frozen in a pose.

"I don't have the words," her mom said. Her face was pushed up close to the camera, the green goo of her face mask not obscuring her pained expression.

"I like it better than the last one," Linda said, her voice uncertain.

Raven looked down at the light wash overalls she'd bought at a boutique in town. She'd added a red flannel shirt underneath to complete the look.

"Okay, I need more, ladies," Raven said. "Give me a word, an adjective."

"Shapeless," her mother offered.

"Rugged," Linda said.

"Jesus, okay, into the no pile this one goes as well," Raven said.

Since deciding to hold out and stay in Cedar Lake for at least the summer, Raven wanted to cement her commitment by purchasing appropriate work attire. Items that said, "I'm a local. I'm from here." But so far, her mother and Linda were not impressed.

"I think it might help if you got ones that fit better," Linda said.

"I agree with Linda. More Dolly Parton, less railroad engineer."

"Well, I got these from the men's section," Raven said. "None of the women's were long or big enough."

"Would it kill traditional men's fashion to adopt strategically placed darts that contour the ass?" her mom asked seriously.

"Okay, that's it. I'm admitting defeat," Raven said. "I think I'll keep the rain jacket and the hiking boots but return everything else."

The older women concurred with Raven's conclusion.

"I gotta head back to the front," Linda said before turning the phone on herself and saying, "It was nice to meet you, Patricia."

"You too, Linda," her mom said. "And I'll definitely send you that flourless chocolate cake recipe."

After Linda had left her room, Raven said, "Oh, I forgot to show you the books I got as well."

She retrieved the tote bag with her purchases from the small bookstore and presented them to her mother.

"They're both business related," Raven explained as if her mother would think books titled *So You Want to Be a Boss… Babe?* and *Girl, Incorporated* were about anything else.

"I can't believe you're doing all this," her mom said with some wonderment. "You're fearless, honey."

"Honestly, I don't know if it's fearlessness or pettiness driving me right now," Raven said. She felt too much satisfaction recalling the vexed look on Silas's face when he realized what was going on.

"I think Chuck would find this whole situation hilarious. He'd appreciate your stubbornness," her mom said.

"You've been thinking about him lately?" she asked, catching the sad smile that crossed her mother's lips.

"A little. For obvious reasons."

"You never told me why you guys broke up," Raven said.

Chuck was the only boyfriend her mom ever introduced Raven to growing up. She hadn't appreciated at the time what a big deal that was.

"Oh, he loved Cedar Lake. Wanted to live there. Work there. And die there. I had you to think of. You had your friends, and I had a good job. We had different priorities."

"Do you regret it?" Raven asked. "Your choice to not leave with him."

"No, it felt right at the time, and who's to say the relationship wouldn't have fallen apart once we got there?"

Her mother's words, while bittersweet, bolstered Raven's decision to stay. The future was unknown, so she might as well fully embrace the journey she'd set upon.

Chapter Six

SILAS HAD no idea what to expect at work on Monday morning as he and the team waited for Raven to arrive in the break room. They were all seated at the table except for Silas, who leaned against a counter, too restless for a chair.

"Maybe she took the weekend and reconsidered," Doc said.

"Doubtful," Halo replied as she stared into the dark well of her coffee mug. Though she'd never admit it, she felt guilty she'd triggered their current situation.

"She can't be spiteful forever, so she won't stay past the summer," Silas said, adopting his brother-in-law's outlook.

When Raven finally showed up, she strode into the kitchen with straight shoulders and a file tucked under her arm. If Silas had any hope that Raven would be okay returning to the busywork he'd given her last week, her assured strut extinguished it.

"Morning," Raven said once she'd placed herself at the head of the table. "First, I want to say it's a brand-new week, so clean slate."

She looked around, meeting each of their eyes: a queen pardoning her subjects.

"I meant it when I said I want to help," Raven said. "So, in that spirit, I have some suggestions to improve things around here."

They all shifted where they sat and stood, and Silas prepared himself to push back on the most disastrous proposals.

"First order of business is getting that sink fixed," she said, reading from a piece of paper she'd pulled from the file.

It was a logical first action. One Silas would've taken when the sink broke weeks ago if he'd had access to the business funds.

"You'll need to change the name on the business bank account to your name to access any money to pay for the plumber," Silas said.

The accounts had been frozen shortly after Chuck's death. Only payroll, which a third party handled, and automated bills continued to be paid as usual. Other auxiliary expenses like gas for the shuttle van and supplies for their different classes were coming straight from his pocket. Silas had planned to reimburse himself once ownership had been sorted out.

"Easy. I'll do that this week," Raven said. "We should also see if we can budget for a new computer and a better appointment scheduling software. The Pilates studio my mom goes to has a really good one."

She continued down her list, proposing other improvements. A few of her ideas had been ones he'd tried to encourage Chuck to adopt for years. But even so, Silas had to fight the impulse to reject every single one of them simply because they were coming from her.

"Also, I have this." Raven pulled out a box covered in

decorative paper with a slot at the top. "It's a suggestion box. If you have any other ideas or feedback, you can drop them here."

Bodie threw his hand in the air as if in school, his muscular arm straining the seams of his T-shirt.

"Yes, Bodie?" Raven said.

"How many suggestions per person?" he asked.

"As many as you can think of," she said.

Bodie pumped his fist. "Hell yeah."

She'd regret that allowance.

In the end, the meeting went better than Silas had expected. Seeing as she wasn't planning on erecting a statue of herself at the front, he thought he could survive her stint here.

The team scattered to different corners of the cabin to prepare for their morning classes, but Raven stopped Silas before he could reach the front door.

"I'd like to come with you on your shuttle pickups today," she said to him. "I heard that Chuck used to do them, so I'd like to learn the route and maybe take that duty off your plate."

Just like everything else involving Raven, this declaration felt like encroachment. But he was an adult. He could play nice and let her take up a responsibility he had no real attachment to.

"We leave in ten," he said.

———

When Silas boarded the shuttle bus, he found Raven seated, assessing herself in a compact mirror. She said nothing, so he didn't either, and they began their trip in silence. It wasn't until they hit the long stretch of road that took them down the mountain that either said another word.

"What did you lose in the wager?" she asked.

He met her eyes briefly in the rearview mirror, cursing the day he made that fucking bet.

"I'm paying for drinks for a month," he said.

"What made you think I couldn't last?"

This line of questioning wouldn't produce anything good. What happened to the clean state? He hesitated before answering, wondering if he should play clueless, but he ultimately decided to tell her the truth. "You have no experience with the outdoor tourism business. Also, people from big cities tend to find Cedar boring long-term."

She didn't respond, and he took her silence to mean concession.

When they arrived at the first inn, Silas pulled up to the entrance and told Raven, "I always get out at each stop and greet the tourists."

They hopped off the bus and found a waiting family of four and an elderly couple decked out in camo that still had the folding lines from the store.

"Morning, everyone," Silas said warmly, but the group replied with lackluster energy.

"Oh, c'mon now, you gotta give me more than that," he said. "That sounded like you think this bus is taking you to Alcatraz."

The joke got the adults chuckling.

"Okay, let's try that again. Morning, everyone!"

"Morning," they spiritedly responded before Silas gave a short introduction. Once the last of the guests had boarded the bus, he turned to Raven and asked, "Simple enough?"

His question was laced with a snark he thought he had

a rein on, but unfazed, Raven responded, "I think I'll manage."

And during the subsequent stops, she proved to be sweet and effervescent, smiling and welcoming everyone with a compliment. "Those are cute sneakers. Look at you in that hat! Now, what vitamins do I need to take to look so awake in the morning?"

It brightened the recipients' countenances immediately.

"How am I doing?" Raven asked him at one point, her brows pinched as if genuinely curious, but she'd actually thrown out a challenge. And for the remainder of the pickups, they were seemingly competing to be the most amiable.

He produced his best smiles, high fives, and the most enthusiastic "Are you ready to have fun?" while she continued to hurl affirmations at everyone.

Who won? Nobody, because they sounded as coherent as banging pots talking over one another.

On their way back up to Mountaintop, Silas watched Raven walk the length of the bus, doing more socializing and laughing with the tourists. She fit in easily. Played the part well. And it fucking irked him.

"So what do you do?" he heard one of the ladies ask Raven.

"I'm the owner," she said as confidently as one would declare the sky blue.

"Oh, the owner," they cooed.

"Yes. Yes," Raven said, grinning from ear to ear.

Irksome.

"Look! Baby bears!" someone shouted midway through their trip.

The black bears were far enough from the road that Silas felt comfortable pulling the van over and allowing photos. The tourists raced to the shuttle's left side, squeezing to find a spot at the wide windows.

When Raven walked up to him in the driver's seat, Silas was studying the time, calculating how many minutes he could spare before they were late.

"Could you take some pictures for me? There's no space back there," she said.

From the clipped tone of her voice, she seemed to resent having to make the request, which may have been the only reason it wasn't painful for him to oblige.

He used her phone and captured the mother bear and her cubs in photos and video.

"Make sure to get all three babies in one picture," Raven said, leaning in to observe his work.

She was close enough to him that he picked up her perfume, and she didn't smell of an overbearing floral fragrance like he might've expected if he'd ever given what she smelt like a thought before that moment. Orange was the dominant note. It was nice.

"Perfect," Raven said, retrieving her phone from him and swiping through the images and clips he'd taken with a soft smile on her lips. "They're so beautiful that you forget they're dangerous animals. Can't imagine just playing dead if one of them attacked."

Something died inside Silas hearing the inaccurate statement expressed so confidently. As much as Raven might play the part of CEO of Mountaintop Adventures well, her expertise was shallow.

"You don't play dead if a black bear attacks you," he told her pointedly. "If you're insisting on owning this business, you should probably know that."

The last part left his mouth without thought, but Raven looked more amused than embarrassed by his call-out. Like his irritation was adorable to her.

"You're a fire sign, aren't you?" she asked, her eyes scanning his face with unnerving intensity.

"W-what?" he asked, thrown by the question and change of subject.

"Yeah, you're a fire sign," she said with a confident nod before walking off and leaving in her wake a lingering orange scent and the impression he'd somehow been insulted.

Chapter Seven

ACCORDING TO ANDREA TELLER, author of *So You Want to Be a Boss... Babe?*, there were rules—102, to be exact—that all women in the workplace should follow to be successful. Some of them Raven found outdated, like rule #5 (avoid too feminine attire), or bizarre, like rule #9 (when at a business lunch, don't chew your food excessively), but she was hoping many would be apt.

For instance, her decision to start doing hotel pickups was initiated by rule #25, a call to display competency. However, the stress involved with maneuvering a big van up and down the mountain and through tight parking lots had aged her at least a decade in the last few days. But she kept at it, partly because she knew Silas was waiting for a reason to declare her unsuitable and resume the duty.

"Knowledge is power. Wield it," Teller wrote in chapter eight, and Raven realized she'd gained a lot of insight into the business last week while answering customer service emails.

She used that information to revamp the website with a

FAQ section and tighten up class and tour descriptions that previously left potential customers confused. She also thought it important to understand what the staff did during the workday, so she announced she'd be joining each of them for at least one of their classes over the coming weeks.

No one was particularly thrilled by this arrangement, and Halo even rolled her eyes. But Raven didn't let any of it dissuade her. And that very afternoon, she joined Bodie for his Fire-making 101 workshop.

While Bodie outside of class was smiley and friendly, Bodie, the survival instructor, was keen and mysterious.

"Fire-making is all about the materials, the technique, and most importantly, the patience," he said to her and five other students before starting his lecture and demonstration.

It was magical to witness how a flame emerged with little effort and a bunch of sticks. Raven was convinced he was Hephaestus in the flesh.

When it was their turn to put the lesson into practice, Raven got on her knees and created a tinder pile in her pit with dry leaves and twigs. She struck her flint with a pocketknife but produced nothing more than the sound of steel against rock. Again and again, she tried, sometimes creating a spark that would vanish along with excitement. The smell of heat on the verge of a flame was in the air, but after twenty minutes of trying, all she had was sweat on her brow and stiff fingers.

Her frustration built with each triumphant yip a fellow novice made when they succeeded in starting a fire. Bodie, however, didn't allow Raven to despair for too long. He crouched in front of her and cupped her hands in his, stopping her frantic attempts.

"You're too tense," he said softly. "You're moving like

you're in control. Fire will come. It's inevitable. Believe that and move with ease."

There was something beautiful about his words, and Raven, now rejuvenated, went through the steps again, slower this time, making it almost a dance she performed. And when she least expected it, a strong spark erupted, igniting the tinder. With shaky hands, she quickly added some kindling and watched the flame grow and grow.

"You've all just made your first fire," Bodie said, bowing over clasped hands.

Raven's confidence boost from the class carried her through the next day when she followed another Andrea Teller recommendation to take work-specific initiative.

She decided to rearrange the front area of the cabin. It was the first space people saw when they came in, and as it currently stood, it did not have a nice flow. Customers spent too long trying to locate the front desk, and if more than one instructor had tourists waiting for them, the cabin got loud and disorderly as everyone tried to parse out who went with who.

She solicited Bodie's help during a midmorning break he had, and while they moved a display case filled with pelts that had belonged to Chuck, he asked, "Where did you learn feng shui?"

"Oh, I'm not an expert at all," Raven said. "But I worked for a realtor who was, and I used to help her set up her show homes."

Next, Bodie and Raven tackled the waiting room setup, moving the chairs farther back in the room and creating designated areas for each guide.

By the time noon arrived, the cabin was more appealing. However, Raven soon found out not everyone shared her opinion.

"What have you done?" Silas asked when he, Halo, and Doc returned to the cabin for lunch.

"I moved some things around."

"Some?" Halo said, mouth agape. "There was nothing wrong with how it was before."

"Well, whenever customers come in, it's not obvious where they should go next," Raven said, pointing to how her new layout fixed that.

"It does get a little confusing in here," Doc said thoughtfully, and Raven's heart leaped at the apparent endorsement.

She'd come to learn that Doc was very levelheaded and smart. His cosign had to mean something to the others.

But Silas dashed those hopes by saying, "This setup would be an immediate fire code violation."

He walked across the room to the back door—the fire exit, where he attempted to open said door, but the motion was impeded by a set of chairs she'd placed there to extend the waiting area.

"Also…" Silas said, moving back to the front entrance to flick the edge of the welcome mat with the toe of his worn boot. "You removed the duct tape. It was ugly but necessary because this is now a tripping hazard."

He then showed how a shelf she'd shifted, mere inches to the right, now blocked access to one of the fire extinguishers affixed to the wall.

Her cheeks grew warm as Silas continued to point out more oversights. The whole situation was made worse by the subtle but present smug look on Halo's face and how Bodie and Doc seemed to be embarrassed on her behalf.

It was all very awkward, but Raven was going to cling to some semblance of her pride, so she did as Teller's rule #16 said and attempted to assert herself.

"Sorry, could I speak with you in private, Silas?" Raven asked, interrupting him mid-critique.

She walked to the storage closet and directed him inside with her hand. He hesitated, and she wondered how she'd respond if he outright refused. But he strode into the room, albeit leisurely.

When she closed the door behind them and finally turned to face him, she said, "I understand that my presence is inconvenient for you, but I need you to show me some respect. If you have a problem with something I've done, pull me aside and let me know like I'm doing now instead of whatever you did out there."

"All right, noted. And I wasn't trying to embarrass you, so I apologize," Silas said. "Anything else?"

She shook her head. "Not unless you have something to get off your chest."

He opened his mouth but quickly shut it.

"No, come on, share your thoughts," she said, tilting her head to meet his face more squarely.

"I have nothing constructive to say."

"Then give me the unconstructive," she said. Maybe if they cleared the air with the unspoken feelings, it'd lessen the weirdness between them.

His jaw worked for a moment before he said, "You annoy me."

"I annoy you? Okay?" She laughed and crossed her arms. "It explains that scary-looking vein that pops out in your neck whenever I speak."

It was his turn to laugh humorlessly. "Is it pride that won't make you accept this isn't your thing?"

"Is it arrogance that makes you think you can tell me what is and isn't my thing?"

"You pretty much admitted that yourself when you gave up."

"I didn't give up."

"You signed the bill of sale."

"And yet I'm still here," she said with a flare of her hands like a game show model introducing a prize.

"This is some summer project to you. I've put blood, sweat, and tears into this place—"

"Wait, is that what was on the shelves in here?" she asked, looking around the storage room she'd cleaned her first day.

An exasperated sound left Silas's mouth in a puff. "Cute."

"Chuck left me this business—"

"On a technicality," Silas said.

"Sure, but it's still the reality, and you've gotta come to terms with it."

"And if I don't?"

"What?" she asked, not expecting his question.

"You gonna fire me if I don't act like you want me to?"

Until that moment, Raven hadn't conceptualized that she even had that kind of authority. She knew she was the "boss," but not with actual, literal power. It tempered some of the adrenaline coursing through her body.

"I'd never," she said emphatically.

The harsh slant of Silas's brows softened slightly, like he too, was recalibrating what all of this meant. What were their roles? How the hell were they supposed to work together when they wanted the same job?

With all this thinking going on, a hush briefly fell between them, and she was now aware of how close they'd drawn. She could feel every exhale from his nose. He smelled like menthol and something else she couldn't immediately identify.

Silas spoke, but she missed what he said, still inexplicably taking inventory of his person. But he was now looking at her intently, the way one does when waiting for a reply. Raven was not interested in admitting she'd been distracted, so she responded with the vaguest retort she could think of: "Whatever."

He didn't have a chance to react before the door to the storage room opened with Halo on the other side. The short woman looked at them both and said, "You know this shit's not soundproof, right?"

Raven winced. She'd definitely broken one of the rules for women in the workplace.

———

Silas had been too smug. Too goading.

He watched Raven leave the storage closet, and he regretted not keeping his thoughts to himself. Not because they were untrue, but because he'd learned in his three decades on earth to lead with tact.

Telling Raven he found her annoying was *not* tactful.

Halo gave him a questioning look because arguing in closets was unlike him. He was the careful one, the steady one. The one Chuck had enlisted to communicate with contractors and local media because of his deft approach. Raven operated differently. She was a destabilizer—she liked to make changes just for the sake of it.

He and Halo left the closet for the break room and found only Bodie and Doc.

"Everything good?" Doc asked, his lips stiff and his brow furrowed.

"Perfect," Silas replied, retrieving his food from the refrigerator before finding a spot at the table.

The others followed suit, but the conversation that usually ensued did not. In its place was the sound of moving furniture from the other room. Raven had seemingly chosen to forgo lunch to restore the cabin's original setup.

Good.

Toward the end of their meals, the sounds in the cabin changed once again with the inflow of afternoon tourists and students. Silas grabbed his archery equipment he stored on a shelving unit between classes and searched for his next client among the throng in the front area. He fleetingly wished for the part of Raven's arrangement that solved this problem.

"Hey, what's up, man," Silas said to his student, Christian, when he finally found him.

"Excited for practice," Christian said, picking up his gear. "Been doing those drills you showed me last time."

Christian was a local who'd been taking private lessons from Silas for about a year. It was a welcomed variety in Silas's weekly schedule that mostly consisted of beginners.

"Let's head out," Silas said, taking a step forward, but Christian stopped his progress with a hand to his chest.

"Hold on, who's that?" Christian asked, nodding to Raven, who was now working the reception.

"Raven. She's here for the summer," Silas said vaguely.

"She's kinda hot," Christian said, his eyes still trained on her, tracking her movements as she spoke with customers at her desk.

Silas cast a look in the same direction to confirm what he'd already been aware of: Raven was an attractive woman. Statuesque and thick was a winning combination, and today she wielded her assets in a pair of high-waisted relaxed jeans and a fitted T-shirt that exposed a sliver of her midriff.

"Pop your eyes back in your head, and let's go," Silas said, nudging the other guy the last steps out the door.

When they arrived at the far end of the field where

Silas held his classes, Christian began his warm-up with some arm mobility rotations as Silas set up his clipboard to take notes.

"Do you know if she's single?" Christian asked, his arm static in a stretch across his body.

"Man, you still on that?" Silas asked.

"What? Am I walking on claimed territory? If you're interested, I'll back off."

"Not even close," Silas said, laughing.

"So, is she single?"

"I have no idea. And weren't you just going on about someone else last week?"

"That's casual," Christian said with a grin. "Nothing wrong with entertaining more than one person if you're safe about it."

Christian worked as a forestry technician for a logging company in town, but he insisted on calling himself a lumberjack. "Ladies love it," he once told Silas. And it was true if his healthy dating life was any indication.

"Whatever, man, but I'm not your matchmaker," Silas said. "My only job here is to train you for that upcoming tournament."

He wouldn't allow Raven to disrupt yet another thing in his life. Selfishly, Silas loved coaching archers who were nerds about the intricacies of the sport, who cared about how a slight mental or physical adjustment affected their shot. It was fun imparting all the stored knowledge he'd accumulated over his career.

Once sufficiently warmed up, Christian started a set at the shooting line with his recurve bow.

"Mind your draw elbow," Silas said after a few shots, and Christian shifted his right arm ever slightly on his next shot. When they moved on to a target farther from the shooting line, Silas said, "Your front alignment is better."

"Thanks, I feel it," Christian said as he settled into a new set. Partway through, however, the wind picked up.

"Fuck, too many sixes," Christian said, studying his less-than-tight arrow grouping.

"Remember to engage your lower body," Silas said, moving his legs into an open stance. "Keep the tension until the end of your shot. It'll reduce the lurching." He picked up his bow to demonstrate, and when his arrow hit the bull's eye, he said, "Make sense?"

"Have you ever thought of competing again?" Christian asked as they traded places. "You're still good even with…" The man's eyes darted to Silas's right shoulder, and he resisted the impulse to rub it.

"I might be perfect on the first shot, the tenth shot, even the fiftieth shot," Silas said, "but I can't guarantee it on the hundredth."

Archery was all about consistency in form and technique, and to achieve that required hours of daily training. Silas couldn't do that anymore because sudden stiffness fucked up his draws, and pain limited the time he could spend in practice.

Pity flashed across Christian's face, but Silas ignored it and the dull ache pressing against his chest. "Okay, let's move this back to sixty meters and see what you got."

Chapter Eight

RAVEN STARED at the sterling faucet, shiny and beautiful, almost scared to breathe near it. She slowly twisted her head to look under the spout—no leaking water.

Ed, the plumber, chuckled from behind. "It's brand spanking new. Won't give out on you for a long time."

"Of course," Raven said, straightening. "I'm a little paranoid, I guess."

He'd spent less than an hour on the job, and a problem that had haunted Raven since her first day was suddenly gone. She tossed the plastic contraption that held the previous faucet together and thanked Ed.

Instead of dashing off to his next client as Raven expected, the plumber took a seat and cradled the glass of water she had offered him earlier.

"How are you getting along in Cedar?" Ed asked after a sip.

"It's a beautiful place. My favorite part of my day is the commute. And I've never said that about any commute before," Raven replied, laughing.

"And Silas? How's he taking you being the new boss?" the man asked, his voice dropping to a stage whisper.

His question was outside of what Raven typically considered small talk, but she supposed a small town would have different criteria.

"Silas has been very accommodating and professional," Raven replied, hoping nothing about her delivery undermined the statement. Because the truth was since her little argument with Silas in the supply closest days ago, they'd been giving each other a wide berth. Curt hellos and good-byes were all they offered one another. If that.

Raven's impulse was always to smooth things over—disharmony made her stomach churn—but she was gritting her teeth and reminding herself why she confronted Silas in the storage closet in the first place.

"Would you say he's been more withdrawn or more visibly frustrated?" Ed asked next, and it was such an odd question that it gave Raven pause.

Ed watched her carefully—like he didn't want to miss her response. He also sat in his chair as if it were out on a deck on a summer's eve. And it became clear to Raven that the plumber was fishing for gossip.

A protectiveness rose in her, not for Silas, but for the business in general. She would not expose them to wagging tongues. Ed had to go.

"We're doing great," she said to the man, gesturing for his now-drained glass. "Transitions are sometimes tricky, but it's going better than I could've hoped."

Within a minute, Raven had Ed out the door, and she felt triumphant, like she'd successfully eliminated a spy trying to bring down a kingdom instead of a nosy man.

It was nearly lunchtime, so Raven returned to the kitchen to beat the queue for the microwave and warm her food. She was standing in front of the appliance, listening to it whir, when Silas entered the break room. They barely made eye contact and didn't exchange a word.

He walked to the other side of the counter, opened a cupboard, and shut it to search another. And another. Until Raven was sure he'd touched every last one twice over.

Tired of the muttering and the banging, she asked him, "Are you looking for something?"

"You moved the coffee filters," he said, damn near glaring at her.

"I reorganized earlier," she blandly responded as she approached the cupboard he stood in front of and tapped the box on the shelf just below his eye line. "I thought it made more sense if they were with the rest of the coffee and tea stuff instead of on top of the refrigerator."

He didn't honor her with any expression of gratitude.

When the rest of the staff showed up, it was to the hum of the percolating coffee maker and a microwave ding. She smiled at them but received muted responses.

"The sink's fixed," Raven said, and they responded slightly more enthusiastically and even tested the faucet.

But as everyone gathered around the table to eat their respective lunches and slog through strained prattle, Raven realized despite paying herself a salary, her name being on the proverbial masthead, and her viewing Mountaintop as hers to protect, she was still not part of the team.

———

"Don't bother with a tray, Kendra," Silas said to the old bartender with a painful-looking sunburn.

She placed four pilsner glasses before him and said, "You better not spill anything on my floor, Reynolds."

It was a funny assertion considering the vinyl floor had

never exactly been clean, but Silas replied, "I wouldn't dare."

Before he could leave, Kendra stopped him with "Oh, what's going on with Mountaintop? I heard the new owner isn't selling."

Silas hoped the news hadn't spread, that he'd own the business before anybody discovered the complications he was facing. But that was wishful thinking in Cedar Lake.

"It's temporary," he said. "A little hiccup. You know, lawyers and paper shuffling."

Clyde, a career sawmill worker and the only person in town Silas felt petite next to, turned from the drink he'd been nursing at the bar and asked, "Chuck didn't leave Mountaintop to you?"

"Not technically. He forgot to change an old will," Silas said.

"Ah, tough break. But chin up, son," Clyde said. "Bad luck doesn't last forever." The big man choked on the last few words, burying his face in his massive hands.

Silas turned to Kendra and lifted a questioning brow, which she responded to by mouthing, "Yara."

Well, that made sense.

Yara and Clyde had been married for two decades but were notorious for splitting up and reconciling every other year. The reasons for the breakups were never clear. Silas patted the big man's back before leaving with his drinks.

With its kitschy neon-lit signs, spacious interior, and reliable service, Blue's was the go-to place locals patronized after work and on the weekends. Silas wove his way through the busy bar toward Mountaintop's usual table at the back.

Doc and Bodie were the only ones seated when he arrived, and they were arguing about Chestnut the squirrel's language acquisition progress.

"You can't tell me that doesn't sound like he's saying hello," Bodie said, pressing his phone to Doc's ear.

"It literally sounds like a bunch of squeaking," Doc replied.

"But the cadence. Hell-o. Hell-o. How can't you hear that?" Bodie asked.

When Halo joined them minutes later, it was with a stronger glower than usual; she'd received a call as they were stepping into the bar.

"Everything okay?" Silas asked Halo as she took a seat on the stool beside him.

"Teenagers. It's fine. Her dad's handling it," Halo said, and she reached for one of the glasses, raising it in the air. "Okay, cheers, everyone. To getting through another busy week."

Once they'd all taken a sip, Bodie asked, "Should we have invited her?"

None of them had to clarify who Bodie was referring to. Silas had not *not* invited Raven; he just hadn't filled her in that they'd be heading to Blue's after work. Plus, he didn't think she'd like the reminder that Silas was paying for the drinks because of a bet made against her.

"I'm going to put it out there that I wouldn't have minded," Bodie said, shrugging. "She's nice. She called me the fire god Hepatitis, so."

"Bud, I think you mean Hephaestus," Doc said.

Bodie blinked. "Hm. Maybe."

"Anyway, I think she's done some cool work around Mountaintop," Doc said.

"Like what? Removing old calendars from the wall?" Halo asked, laughing.

"I guess you guys haven't seen the website, then," Doc said.

"The website?" Silas asked.

"Yeah, she changed it. Made it actually look good," Doc said, grabbing his phone and pulling up Mountaintop's site for Silas and Halo to see.

Silas could tell within seconds of scrolling that Raven had completely revamped the site. The previously dry and minimal page now had accent colors, their logo, and animation. She'd also added notes to each of the classes and tours they provided, disclosing the level of physical exertion one could expect.

It was a fantastic addition because sometimes tourists didn't realize they'd be participating in physically demanding activities. Then there were the separate pages she'd included that addressed accessibility, accommodations, and frequently asked questions.

"It's good," Halo said with blatant awe.

"Yeah," Silas said, but the more accurate description was "excellent."

It felt odd to admire something Raven had done when he'd spent all his time since meeting her resentful about her presence. But it was also just a website. It didn't mean she was fit to run Mountaintop. He knew that, and hopefully she'd realize that too.

"I was thinking of asking her to do the band's site," Doc said with an inflection that made the statement sound like a question. Silas might've dismissed the moment if not for everyone turning to look at him.

It *was* a question. Specifically, a request for permission.

Silas tensed. His brother had told him not to let Raven get under his skin, but she had, and he'd telegraphed that irritation to the team to the point where they thought he needed absolute fealty.

"Listen, man, you're free to do whatever you want," Silas said, desperately hoping they'd all take that to heart.

But as the evening progressed, the group's reaction

continued to nag him, and he decided he'd douse whatever annoyances Raven stirred. He needed to foster a work environment where people weren't walking on eggshells.

———

There was a bug chewing on Raven's exposed ankle, and for half a minute, she furiously shook her leg, trying to get rid of it, only to realize it was a leaf caught in her sock all along.

"You okay?" a woman beside Raven asked.

"I'm great," Raven replied, regaining her composure.

They were on the last mile of Doc's five-mile forest walking tour, and Raven could honestly say if she disregarded the spider web she'd walked into face-first on mile one, the tumble she'd almost taken in mile two, and the blister currently forming on her left big toe, she'd enjoyed herself.

In no small part to Doc's wealth of knowledge and dry humor.

For instance, at the beginning of the tour, a man asked Doc, "Does your name mean something in your language?"

"Yes, but I can't say. It's sacred," Doc had replied, his sarcasm going undetected by the tourist, who nodded with apparent understanding.

As they neared the end of the tour, Doc paused to recap points he'd made the last ninety minutes.

"Remember always to look up," Doc said. "The trail blazes on the trees will be your best guide."

"What happens if you miss a marker and get lost?" someone asked.

"Backtrack," Doc replied. "If that doesn't work and you're completely disoriented, the first thing to do is not panic. Stay put because if you've informed someone of your hiking plans beforehand, which you always should, people will eventually come looking. Don't make that job harder by aimlessly wandering. If there's a need for you to move because of danger, head downhill. That's where a body of water that leads to a road will be."

The group completed the final kilometers of the trail and emerged from the forest. The cabin was visible in the distance, and so was Silas, who was wrapping up a class. Not much had changed between them except that his "Good morning" that day didn't sound quite as terse as usual.

At some point, as Raven crossed the field, she found herself walking side by side with Doc. "That was a really cool experience," she told him.

"Thanks," he simply said, and she assumed they'd finish the trek in silence, but he continued, "By the way, I like what you've done with Mountaintop's website."

"Oh my God, thank you," Raven said, beaming at the unexpected compliment. "I was nervous about it, so I'm happy you like it."

She'd been wading through her time at Mountaintop without knowing if her contributions were making an impact beyond inconveniencing Silas.

"No, yeah, it's great," Doc said. "I've been wanting to ask if you'd be interested in doing the website for the band I play in. Of course, we'd pay you."

"Hell yeah. I'd be happy to, but no need to pay me. I'm not a professional web designer or anything."

This seemed to bother him, so Raven suggested he give her a ticket to the band's next gig, and they called it even.

As they neared the cabin, Raven spotted litter strewn on the grassed area in front, so she diverted from the path to collect it.

"Why do this?" Raven mumbled to herself while picking up empty fruit cups and granola wrappers. They had many signs asking patrons to dispose of their trash properly and bins all over the property. "Hard to miss," she said, tapping the placard as if the culprits were there to receive the reprimand.

While straightening from a bend, Raven caught something flutter in her peripheral.

Another piece of trash, she naïvely thought. She might've said it was a tuft of dead grass if she were given another chance to guess. But she would've also been incorrect.

It was not more trash or even grass that twitched three feet away from where she stood, but a skunk, with its signature black and white coloring, fussing over something on the ground.

A sound, a unique blend of a gasp and croak, left Raven's mouth as she froze in place.

The animal remained unaware or unconcerned with her, though.

Laughter drew Raven's attention to her left, and she saw Silas talking with a client nearby. He faced her direction, so she bore her eyes into him, hoping he'd look her way.

Nothing.

"Silas," she whispered, also to no avail.

With her limbs anchored by timidity, Raven imagined herself calcifying and remaining there for eternity, but Silas's gaze eventually found hers.

It took a frown, a questioning tilt of his head, and several more brutal seconds before he completely assessed her plight and approached with urgent footfall.

"What do I do?" she whispered through clenched teeth.

"Slow steps to your left," he said, and with much effort and grit, she inched her way toward him.

"That's it," he said. "One step at a time."

But some hostile force must've been hell-bent on making her day miserable because the cabin door opened and customers burst out, chatting and laughing. Silas tried to quiet them, but they were wasted attempts.

"A skunk!" someone shouted, and cries of distress erupted. They all retreated into the cabin, leaving Raven, with reflexes no match for the frightened animal's, to receive a spritz as light as a morning breeze but the olfactory impact of a sucker punch.

Chapter Nine

RAVEN HEARD Silas call her name from somewhere in front of her as she was doubled over, coughing, choking, retching, spitting. Her throat burned, her eyes stung, and she wished for a meteor to hit and end it all.

But Silas's voice was persistent, and it yanked her from her hopeless spiral.

"Help me," she said in a pathetic little voice.

"You've gotta listen. Don't fucking touch your eyes," he said. "I'll be right back."

There was more talking, more commotion, but Raven was too focused on surviving the next breath to bother with interpretation.

Silas returned to her after a time and said, "I'm going to need you to open your eyes and walk to my truck."

She pried open her lids, finding the sun had suddenly become too bright, but she zeroed in on Silas, who was gesturing for her to walk.

On wobbly legs, she followed him to his vehicle, where he instructed her to sit in the passenger seat covered in a tarp. All the windows, including the sunroof, were open.

When they started moving, it didn't dispel the stench of rotten eggs and cabbage as much as it convinced her she'd never smell anything else again.

"Are we going to the hospital?" she asked Silas, whose head was in threat of decapitation the way he drove with it out of the window.

"You're not dying, Raven."

"Honestly, for a second or two back there, I'd have preferred that."

"You need to get the smell off with a bath, that's all," he said.

"We're going to need a lot of tomato juice," she said, already steeling herself.

"No tomato juice. That's an old wives' tale."

"Where are you taking me?" she asked.

"My place."

And what a place it was. Raven didn't know what she was expecting, but she arrived at a beautiful bungalow with a perfectly kempt lawn. Silas kept his distance as he guided her to the back of his house.

"Stand right here," he said, pointing to the corner of the porch. "Don't touch anything."

He disappeared through the glass sliding doors into his home, and with each passing moment, she felt herself become one with the funk. When Silas returned with a large garbage bag, she was thinking about her chances of survival if she flayed her skin.

"Okay, take off your clothes and put them in the bag," he said.

"See, whenever I've heard those words from a random man, I've been at least a few shots deep into a bottle of tequila and can find the humor in it."

"You're not stepping into my house with those clothes on," he said before turning away from her. "Go ahead."

Raven stared at his broad back for many seconds, and no muscle twitched. She tilted her head to the side to look at his face; his eyes were shut.

"Raven," he said, his voice low. "The longer you wait, the harder it gets to neutralize the scent."

"Fuck me," she said as she began undoing and removing her clothing. "Your neighbors are going to get a real show today."

"I promise they can't see you," he said.

Her eyes scanned his yard, and she found his statement supported. A tall fence and dense trees concealed the interior of his backyard.

When she'd taken off all her clothes, she said, "Done."

"Underwear too," he replied.

And she ruefully laughed as she removed the remaining articles and felt the air touch places it had only touched once while skinny-dipping in the dead of night years ago.

"Okay, I'm completely naked," she said. "What's next?"

"You're going to step into my living room through the door behind you, go down the hallway on the right, and walk till you reach the bathroom on your left without a door. Let me know when you're there."

"Wait, why doesn't your bathroom have a door?" she asked.

"I'm in the middle of some renovations."

Great, she thought. Now she was concerned she'd step on a rusty nail. She entered his home, her arms covering her body as she quickly tiptoed through the unfamiliar house.

"I'm in!" she shouted once submerged in the tub.

Moments later, Silas said, from somewhere in the hallway, "You need to be in there for at least twenty minutes."

A long silence followed, and it wasn't clear if Silas was

still in the hallway until he said, "We should probably squash this tension between us. It's not good for the work environment."

"Yeah, okay," she said, unable to dismiss the little respect she gained for him for thinking of the others. Besides, any annoyance Raven wanted to harbor could not be maintained in her current condition.

"Moving forward, we are cordial and friendly," he said.

"Cordial and friendly," she agreed.

There was a sigh and some rustling as he took a seat on the carpeted hallway floor. Raven craned her neck to see past the doorless hole in the wall but could only make out the toes of his socks.

"So, how's your day been?" he asked.

"Go to hell," she said, a laugh finding its way out of her. It was the first laugh they'd shared, and it should have felt weirder than it did. It was a nice release, especially after the last half hour.

"The temperature good?"

"Manageable. What did you put in here?" she asked, slicing her hand through the cloudy water.

"Baking soda."

"That's it? And this will work?" she asked.

"Yeah, my old man is a retired vet, and this is what he'd do for his animal patients and once when my brother got skunked."

"You've lived here your entire life, then," she said.

"Born and raised, but I did leave for a few years."

"Where did you go?" she asked.

"Here and there," he replied.

"No specific locales?" she asked. "What? You part of some organized crime syndicate you can't talk about?"

He made an amused snort.

"Is that how you financed this huge house?" she

continued, taking in the bathroom counter space she only could conjure on Pinterest.

"It's only 1300 square feet."

"Ha! Only 1300," she said. "Please, you should've seen my old apartment. I loved it, but I couldn't turn in my kitchen without bumping an appliance. Like I've never seen a bathtub this big."

She'd be enjoying the rare ability to fully stretch her legs in a tub if she weren't soaking in swill.

"That's a new addition. The reason I had to remove the door," he said. "What do you think of the light fixtures?"

It sounded like he genuinely wanted to know. Not because her opinion specifically mattered but rather because he inquired about everyone's opinion to gauge his taste.

"They're artfully vintage, and I think it works well with the neutral wallpaper," she said, surveying more of the bathroom before something truly bizarre caught her eye. "Why is there a framed picture of your head badly photo-shopped onto a white man's body?"

His sudden burst into boisterous laughter startled her, and as he continued to laugh, she couldn't help but feel delighted in anticipation for the yet-revealed joke.

"Are you going to respond or leave me to draw my own conclusions?"

"It's the main guy from that '90s Robin Hood movie. It was a gag gift from my brother. I forget it's even there."

"Is that what got you interested in archery?"

"I don't think I had seen it before I started taking lessons. I found the sport after attending a fair in town. There was a very basic archery range with shitty arrows and bows. Got hooked and started going to a range an hour out of town."

His voice sounded brighter than she'd ever heard; it held a sense of wonderment no one could fake.

"You love it," she said.

"I do," he replied.

"I'm always fascinated by people who have one passion," she told him.

"You don't?" he asked.

"I like a lot of things. Too many things, some people say. But I guess I feel like I only have a short time on this earth. Why not try out everything?"

"You've had a lot of jobs, then."

"Yeah, I've been a secretary at all sorts of businesses. Medical, tech, construction, you name it. I've done hand modeling —"

"Hand modeling?"

"Yeah, you know, if you're selling jewelry or nail polish, you need hands and limbs to showcase the products. Also worked as a nail technician, a nanny, an acupuncturist, water safety instructor."

"And you've loved and been fulfilled by all of them?" he asked skeptically.

"No, of course not. Some were just jobs, and I've had my fair share of bad ones, like this one personal assistant position for a lady with a bad reputation in media. She was very particular about everything, and she used to order this salad from an upscale bistro—cost like eighteen bucks for the smallest portion imaginable, but she didn't like the feta cheese that came with it. And if the cook forgot to leave it out, I'd have to remove it by hand."

"No way," Silas said.

"Yup, I'd sit at my desk with a toothpick and a teaspoon, removing crumbly feta cheese from a salad."

"Nah, that's too much," he said.

"It was my job. And the money—well, the money was shit, but I got paid."

"I guess I'm lucky or privileged or whatever. I've never had a bad job. I have had a bad day on a job, though," he said before he laughed lightly. "I worked at the ice cream parlor in the summers as a teen, and one day the soft serve ice cream machine malfunctioned—"

"Oh, no," Raven said as she leaned over the tub, already predicting the direction of the story.

"Yeah, my coworker disappeared, there was a growing queue, and here's the machine that won't stop running. So I'm there whipping out cones and bowls as fast as I can, trying to catch the ice cream. At some point, I pull out a bucket. And all anyone could see was some chubby kid on the verge of tears and a lot of wasted ice cream."

Laughter took over, and it was a while before either of them realized the timer had gone off.

———

Silas vacated the hallway, leaving Raven to drain the tub and take a proper shower. As he entered the kitchen, he registered the smile still on his lips. He and Raven had addressed the tension, so the pleasant conversation that came afterward was more than he could've hoped for.

He could admit it had been hard for him to understand the kind of adult who'd, on a whim, drop their regular life to spend the summer doing a job they'd never been interested in. But in those twenty minutes, Silas gleaned Raven's love of life. He could appreciate her audacity even if it was still confounding and—honestly—scary. What would it be like to make potentially life-altering decisions without fear?

Listening to Raven speak had also inadvertently given

him hope she'd leave; he knew Cedar would never satisfy the wanderer in her.

Silas busied himself creating a simple cheese board for Raven. He wasn't sure she'd want to eat anything, but it felt like the natural thing to do. Something he'd want.

The sound of running water eventually stopped, and Raven appeared in the kitchen shortly thereafter with her braids wrapped inside a towel, her face bare, and wearing a slightly baggy T-shirt and a pair of sweatpants he'd left for her.

It was striking to see her this pared down. Had her eyes always been that big? He realized he was staring and offered her a seat at his breakfast table.

"Is this for me?" she asked, looking at the board he'd assembled as she settled into her chair.

"You don't have to eat it. I just threw it together in case," he said, suddenly feeling sheepish about the effort.

"No, it looks good, thank you," she said.

"Would you like something to drink? Sparkling water, regular water, iced tea?"

"Sparkling water would be great," she replied, and Silas grabbed a can from the refrigerator and poured it into a glass with some ice. When he turned to deliver, he found Raven fixing the drooping towel around her hair. Her arm placement caused the shirt to press against her full breasts, revealing the outline of her hardened nipples and the piercing in one of them.

Silas almost dropped the glass he held.

"Careful," Raven said, reaching for her drink.

And as she delighted in the light pomegranate flavor of her drink, Silas dealt with the heat sweeping across his body by standing against his counter where he could catch a breeze from the open window.

"What type of cheese is this?" Raven asked, lifting a

white cheese wedge with a faint, dark stripe down the middle. "It's good."

"Morbier," he replied in a thankfully strong and steady voice, then added, "There's a legend that says that line was created from ash that was blown in while the cheese was being made."

"Oh, that's beautiful," she said, taking another look at the cheese, and he was oddly glad she appreciated that random piece of knowledge.

"Thank you for all of this," she said.

"Yeah, no problem."

"I'll need to check if Hallmark has a greeting card for the occasion when someone lets you soak in their tub after a skunk has sprayed you."

"If they do, it won't be in stock at Cedar's grocery store," he said, "but if you're itching to sign something to show your gratitude, I have something in mind."

A smile lifted her lips. "You'd need to save me from the literal jaw of a bear for me to consider that."

"Wow, steep price," he said.

"The best I can do is upgrade you from mortal enemy to asshole. You'd join the ranks of my third-grade teacher, an ex, and people who don't put shopping carts back."

"I was at mortal enemy level? I only have you at bane of my existence," he said, his own smile emerging.

"You're also part of some criminal enterprise, so you can't expect me to be the worst person you know."

Before he could volley something back, his doorbell sounded, and Silas found himself irritated at the interruption as he quickly moved to answer the door.

"You okay? I didn't expect to see your truck out front in the middle of the day," his brother-in-law said from the front stoop. He held a basket of apricots he'd most likely planned to leave on the step for Silas.

"Yeah, I'm fine. A coworker got skunked, so I brought her here to—"

"Oh, Halo's here?" Victor asked, moving his head to see inside.

"No, Raven."

Victor's eyes widened. "*The* Raven?"

"You don't need to put 'thee' before her name. She's not some legendary figure."

"Can I meet her?"

"Why?"

"Why not?" Victor countered.

Not interested in shrouding Raven in a mystery that would only serve to pique curiosity further, Silas moved aside to grant his brother-in-law access inside his home.

He introduced the two, and they exchanged pleasantries.

"He's here dropping off fruit," Silas explained.

"I have a garden," Victor said. "Never thought I'd be the type, but it helps with writer's block."

"Oh, you're a writer?" Raven said, which led them to talk about that for a while.

"How's everything going? Running the business and so on," Victor asked carefully, the underlying question evident.

"Well, I'm the bane of his existence, and I think he's an asshole, so better than last week," Raven said.

And as his brother-in-law's laughter filled the room, she turned to Silas and winked, sending an unexpected thrum across his chest.

Chapter Ten

RAVEN WOKE UP WITH A START, the remnants of her dream lingering in unspecific sequences. Sweat-slick limbs, tangled sheets, mouths hanging open on sounds of ecstasy, her and Silas in the titular roles.

"Fuck," she said as she pushed the covers off her body and sat up in bed.

She was going to blame the skunk situation from yesterday. The hours she'd spent in his home had felt intimate—like the morning after a hookup. She'd been wearing his clothes, her hair wet, her face bare. He'd even prepared her food like they were famished from fucking.

It was no wonder her subconscious had decided to have fun and imagine her in the most illicit positions with him, but now wide-awake, she felt strange, not to mention aroused. She stepped into the shower and ran the water as cold as she could stand it, hoping it would excise the images from her mind as she scrubbed her body.

It was somewhat successful, but she was glad she had the weekend to reset before facing Silas.

Once dressed and groomed, she walked to the motel

head office to complete her weekend chores. She found Linda behind the lobby desk talking with the florist, Kriti, who ran a flower shop with her father and dropped off an order every few days.

"Hi, ladies," Raven said as she approached the women. "Sorry I'm late, Linda. I had quite the day yesterday."

"What happened?" Linda asked, concerned.

"I got skunked on the Mountaintop property."

"Ah, shit. Sneaky pests, those ones," Linda said with a tsk.

Kriti leaned toward Raven and sniffed. "I can't tell. You smell fresh as a daisy."

"I better. I've showered five times since yesterday. I'm really getting a crash course in Mother Nature up here."

"If you were going to stay through the winter, you'd get the real lesson," Kriti said, laughing.

"Well, who knows? I might still be here," Raven said.

Kriti cocked her head. "Oh? Word around town is that you're leaving before the summer is up."

In her short time in Cedar Lake, Raven had witnessed how gossip traveled. From working in the motel lobby for an hour or so every day, she'd learned about the Tamborskis' daughter's elopement and a growing guinea pig population in Stan Mulligan's backyard that was close to spurring county intervention. She knew she had to nip misinformation in the bud.

"It's not true," Raven said. "There's a very good chance I might stay."

"That would be nice. I think you'd fit right in," Kriti said, and as Raven cleaned and reset the coffee station, her mind kept returning to the fact that Silas, maybe even the others at Mountaintop, were going around town, reassuring locals of her inevitable departure.

The thought had the effect she'd hoped the cold

shower would have had. It was a good reminder for Raven that she was here for business. And at that moment, she— for pride's sake—needed to underscore her intention to make a decision independent of Silas's wants.

"Hey, now that I think about it," Raven said, interrupting Linda and Kriti again, "do you know any realtors? I should start looking into more permanent housing options."

———

Silas was partway through installing high shelves in his living room when his brother showed up.

"Looking good," Isaiah said, taking in the space.

"Thanks. I'm thinking of displaying some of my medals and trophies up there when it's done," Silas said before gesturing to the large box his brother held. "What's in there?"

"Everything you'll need to make customized party favor bags," his brother said.

"How many people are you expecting at this party again?" Silas asked as he inspected the inside of the packed box.

"Please direct any questions you have to Victor. I'm just following instructions," Isaiah said with all the resignation of a man who would've been content with a small backyard party. "Speaking of my husband, he said he met Raven the other day."

"He did."

"Said she was really lovely."

"She is," Silas responded.

"Called her pretty too."

"Sure, yes," Silas casually said, but he had considered this previously inconsequential fact one too many times since she'd come over. Her upswept eyes, the shape and tone of her lips, the curves that made up her soft body. That fucking nipple piercing.

"Victor also said—"

"Jesus, did he perform a monologue?" Silas asked.

Undeterred by the sarcasm, Isaiah continued, "He also said that Raven seemed sociable and warm. Not like someone who was having a difficult time adjusting."

"Okay? What are you trying to say?" Silas asked, taking a seat on the armrest of his sofa.

"Have you thought about what you'd do if Raven remains the owner from now until the foreseeable future?" Isaiah asked, his brows and voice pinched.

"No, I'm not worrying about that right now," Silas said.

"But don't you think preparing for the worst-case scenario would be wise?" his brother asked.

He thought Silas had his head in the sand, scared to face possible realities, but it wasn't true.

"You remember those months after the accident?" Silas asked.

Isaiah took a breath and nodded. "Yeah. They were bad."

A year out from one of the biggest moments in his professional life, he'd decided, on a reckless impulse, to get on an off-highway vehicle known for its lack of lateral stability and crush protection. For his foolishness, he'd sustained a serious rotator cuff injury.

Countless hours of physiotherapy yielded a lot of improvement—he could still shoot—but that wasn't enough in the world of competitive archery.

"I couldn't stomach reading industry news for over a year," Silas said to his brother. "I couldn't imagine ever wanting to pick up a bow again. But I did. So trust me, I know how to make lemonade out of lemons."

"I get it, brother," Isaiah said. "For now, Mountaintop is your sugar."

"Exactly."

———

Over the weekend, Raven had done a good job of diminishing the relevancy of the little dream she had of Silas, or so she thought. When she arrived at Mountaintop the morning of a new workweek, she had a passing discomfort when she found Silas alone in the break room.

"Would you like some?" Silas asked her, the coffee pot in his hand.

Raven blotted out the image of him taking her against an armoire and said, "Thanks, that'd be great."

She watched him prepare her mug, surprised when he got her sugar and creamer preferences correct without asking. "You know how I take my coffee."

"You like an obscene amount of sugar," he lightly said, handing her the cup. "It's hard not to notice."

"Okay, chill, Mr. Judgey. In my defense, the coffee here is shit," she said, taking a relaxed stance against the counter as he had.

"That's on you now," he said. "Actually, where's that suggestion box you made? I should put in an official request for better coffee."

She rolled her eyes as he chuckled, and a comfortable moment followed, which Raven was relieved to experience. There'd been a fear in the back of her head that maybe their agreement to be cordial and friendly wouldn't survive beyond his home. But it seemed like the tension of her early days at Mountaintop was over.

"I used the soap you gave me all weekend," she said.

Without warning, Silas took a step toward her and inhaled deeply. "It worked. All I smell is oranges."

The timbre of Silas's voice reverberated over her exposed skin, and briefly, before he restored the distance between them, Raven regarded his lips. Lush and full. She bet they felt amaz—

"How do you want to go about this?" Raven asked, shoving aside her wayward thoughts.

"About what?"

"Telling the team we're cordial and friendly now."

"I thought we could just show them by being cordial and friendly," he said.

"That would take too long to notice. I want high vibes as soon as possible."

"Okay," he said. "What's your suggestion?"

"We should officially announce it."

"Like an edict," he replied.

"It doesn't have to be all 'Hear ye! Hear ye!' Just a casual update when we're all together."

"You're the boss, so do what you think is right," he said with a lifted hand of surrender.

"Wow, you said that with none of the vitriol I expected."

"What can I say? I've been practicing."

Movement at the door made both of them turn that way. The others had unknowingly arrived and were watching them. Their expressions slack as if they'd walked into a lab and discovered clones of themselves. Presumably, because she and Silas were actually talking.

"Morning," Raven said to break the silence.

But it didn't jolt them out of their stupor, so Silas dramatically cleared his throat and said, "Hear ye! Hear ye! Raven and I have decided to be friendly and cordial."

"Just like that?" Halo asked, brows pulled in.

"Yeah, he practically threw an olive branch at me," Raven said with an exaggerated shrug.

"Well, you got skunked," Silas said, a smile briefly appearing on his face. "It would've been cruel not to offer you the comfort of being in my good graces."

"A philanthropist, folks," Raven said.

Halo and Doc still seemed skeptical about the changeup, but Bodie approached Raven and Silas with a megawatt smile. "I'm happy as a clam in chowder about this," he said before opening his muscular arms and pulling the three of them into a group hug.

"What is chowder? Is it technically a soup?" Halo asked from the other side of the room where she was storing her belongings.

"Yeah, it's just a thick soup," Doc said.

"What's chili then?" Halo asked as everyone congregated around the table.

"Chili is chili," Bodie said.

Unconvinced, Halo pulled out her phone. "Hey, Siri. What is soup?"

The conversation topic continued and revealed passionate opinions, but Raven felt a calm settle over her. Relaxed chatter had returned. It gave her hope that things would only go up from there.

————

When Silas entered the cabin midmorning, Raven's spirited laugh was the first thing he heard. She stood behind the reception, setting up their new office computer and talking to Christian.

Silas shouldn't have been surprised to see his client flirting with Raven because he'd barely been able to shut up about her the last time. And Christian was definitely flirting. His chest was puffed out, and he flexed his bicep every time he went to sweep his hair back.

They didn't immediately acknowledge him, so Silas politely stood there.

"A lumberjack, huh? Does that mean you chop wood in plaid?" Raven asked as she stapled the papers in her hand.

"Sometimes, but that's my regular wardrobe," Christian said with another hair-rake-arm-flex combo, and Silas wondered if Raven was actually receptive or simply humoring Christian.

"You ready go?" Silas asked, interrupting the conversation.

The two turned as if just noticing Silas, and the smile Raven gave him had his palms tingling.

It was a few days into Operation Cordial and Friendly, and the morale around the cabin and among the staff had improved, but Silas was also blaming the new dynamic for all the looking he was doing. He found himself cataloging what exactly he found alluring about Raven on a particular day. Today it was the high ponytail that exposed the elegant column of her neck and the shiny berry color on her lips.

"Give me one second. I have something to ask Ray," Christian said.

Ray? They were on shortened-names basis?

"Are you single?" Christian asked Raven as he leaned over the desk separating them.

Something in Silas's stomach rolled.

"Why? You trying to ask me out, Christian?" Raven said, her voice dropping.

"I'd be a fool not to," he replied smoothly, and she offered the man one of her pretty smiles. "There's a nice place called Bennigan's Steakhouse. I'd like to take you there."

Bennigan's Steakhouse? Silas hated the hell out of that place, with their shit chipotle sauce and tendency to over-cook every dish. You'd only take someone there if you wanted to work on your Heimlich maneuver when they inevitably choked on a tough piece of brisket.

"What?" Christian asked Silas, turning to him, and Silas realized he'd harrumphed very obnoxiously.

With no way to play it off as a clearing of his throat, Silas diplomatically said, "Bennigan's isn't my favorite, that's all."

"Well, it's mine, and it's great," Christian said to Raven. "So what do you say? Have dinner with me?"

"I can't," she replied with a sympathetic head tilt, and the tension in Silas's jaw he'd not noticed building relaxed. "I've got a lot on my plate right now," she explained.

"You're killing me here, Ray."

"I'm sorry," she said. "But if I'm here in the fall, and you're still interested, ask me again."

"Oh, I will," Christian said, tapping the table as if his hand were a gavel and he was making his intentions legitimate.

"Good to go now?" Silas asked.

"Yeah, let me use the washroom real quick, though," Christian said.

When he disappeared down the hallway, Raven wildly gestured toward the electronic mess on her desk and said, "Okay, now to finish this."

"How's the setup going?" he asked, stuffing his hands in his pockets as he tried to ignore the sway of her hips as she moved about.

"I'm hopeful I can get it up and running early this

afternoon," she said before she ducked under the table to fiddle with wiring.

Silas could've called out goodbye and waited for Christian outside, but he unexplainably stayed put.

"What's your favorite place?" she asked when she popped back up.

"Sorry?"

"You said the steakhouse wasn't your favorite, so what is?"

"There's a Brazilian restaurant an hour out of town that I like," he replied.

"Huh, I don't think I've ever had Brazilian food," she said, pausing in her work.

"Unacceptable. You need to fix that as soon as possible."

She looked at him and slowly smiled. "You're not trying to ask me out too, are you?"

Her question was obviously in jest, but it threw him. He struggled to come up with an appropriate response.

"Oh, I was kidding," Raven said, her eyes widening. "I know you weren't—"

"Yeah, no, I got it. I didn't think you were..." Silas said quickly, and before he had to consider how to fill the awkward silence, Christian reappeared.

"Have a great class," Raven said to them, and Silas acknowledged her farewell without meeting her eye.

Chapter Eleven

RAVEN WATCHED Silas from the front window of the cabin as he taught a class. She couldn't make much out from where she stood beyond identifying him from his stature and clothes, but he held her attention.

"Are you going to get that?" Halo asked and brought Raven back to the present where the photocopier she was standing in front of was blinking and beeping for more paper.

Raven quietly chided herself as she fed fresh sheets into the tray.

"Whatchu looking at anyway?" Halo asked, joining Raven to peer out of the window.

"She's looking at Silas. She's been doing it all morning," Libby, Halo's fifteen-year-old daughter, said from her place at the front reception.

"What? No, I've been photocopying," Raven said urgently, holding up the still-warm documents as proof.

But Libby scoffed. It was the teen's second day accompanying her mother to work; she'd returned to Cedar Lake when typical teen rebellion had made remaining at her father's home hours away impossible. She was now finishing online summer school at her mother's.

"Okay, well, it's lunchtime, Libby," Halo said to her daughter. "Your food's in the refrigerator."

"Whoopee," the teen said, getting up. "My second state-sanctioned meal of the day."

The girl stalked off, headphones firmly in place, and Halo turned to Raven and asked, "How was she?"

Since Raven had been tasked with keeping an eye on Libby while Halo was teaching, she had gone from public enemy number one to charitable babysitter.

"Fine, she didn't say much. She did her work and sketched."

"Good. Good. Okay," Halo said, appearing meek with her hands in her pockets.

"This might not be helpful or anything," Raven said, "but I know it's hard right now with her. I'm a daughter of a single mom, and I can tell you, she won't be like that forever. The rules will make sense one day, and she'll appreciate what you've done for her."

Halo's chin wobbled for a moment, but she quickly stiffened it and said, "Thank you."

The older woman left for the break room, and Raven quickly checked her face in her compact mirror in preparation for an interaction with Silas.

Over the last few days, she'd failed to quash her growing attraction to him. However, she'd been maintaining professionalism and avoiding the flirtation that wanted to leap out whenever he was near.

When Silas finally entered the main office, his face peppered with sweat from the warm day, she called him over to talk business.

"What's up?" he asked, joining her where she stood behind the front desk.

"I've been transferring our client list to the new program and noticed something strange with this account's payment record," she said, pointing to figures on the computer.

Silas bent over the table to look, and Raven found herself studying him.

Beautiful thick beard. Solid neck. Nice earlobes. Was there such a thing as nice earlobes?

"Don't worry about that one," he said, straightening.

"Wait, hold on. Why?"

"That's the Crawleys' account. We ignore any of their outstanding balances."

"Why do we do that?" she asked. "Those are several high-amount invoices spanning the last three years."

"The Crawleys are the richest family in Cedar," Silas said, taking a seat on the edge of her desk. "They only live here part-time, but they own pretty much everything worth something in this town."

"I'm still not hearing an explanation for why they're not paying their bills."

"They may be rich," Silas said, "but they're also entitled and don't think they should pay for anything. They'll book an expedition for their son's bachelor party or business retreats without hesitation."

"Do other businesses in town go along with this as well?"

Silas smiled before shouting, "Hey, Bodie!"

"Yes?" the brawny man replied, popping his head out of the break room.

"What are the two rules of Cedar?"

"Never step foot into the marsh near the lake, and don't expect the Crawleys to pay for anything," Bodie said as if by rote.

"But that's ridiculous," Raven said once Bodie had retreated. "If they have the money, they should pay."

"I agree," Silas said. "But unless we want to make it a big deal—and we don't—we take the loss on the chin and hope they don't have more than one occasion a year they want to use our services for."

Raven could recognize that the Crawleys were throwing their weight around, and they wouldn't be the first powerful people to do so. But it bothered her more than it should have, maybe because Cedar Lake seemed too homey for such games.

"What if I talked to them?" Raven asked.

"You'd be wasting your time," Silas said plainly. "And I can't stress enough how much you don't want to offend them."

"Yeah, yeah," she said, waving him off. "I got it."

But she now was determined to get this sorted out.

––––––––

When Raven brought up the Crawleys earlier in the week, Silas assumed that would be the end of the conversation. He thought he'd adequately conveyed why trying to get the richest family in Cedar to pay their bills was a bad idea, but apparently not.

Because as the team was all settling in to have lunch that day, Raven announced, "I made an appointment with the Crawleys to discuss their outstanding bills."

Chatter ceased.

Silas had managed over the last few days to avoid regarding Raven for too long, but her words made it impossible.

"Technically, I'm meeting only with Mr. Crawley, but good enough, right?" she said with a shrug.

"He's coming here to discuss payments?" Halo asked.

"No, I'm going to his house," she said, and riotous laughter erupted.

"What's so funny?" Raven asked.

"The Crawleys don't pay for anything in this town," Doc said, wiping the tears from his face.

"I saw the missus pay for cotton candy once at the rodeo," Bodie said.

"I'm sure that was the same year that out-of-town camera crew came to do the story on that barrel racer," Halo said.

"It was!" Bodie replied, and there was another round of laughter.

"How did you even get a meeting with him?" Silas asked.

"I called the number we have for them in our system and asked the assistant who picked up if I could make an appointment."

Silas was a little in awe with Raven's fearlessness, but of course it was born of ignorance.

"I would cancel," Bodie said.

"Not an option. The meeting's today after work. And I'm going."

Another stunned silence swept the room before Halo said, "If you pull this off, I'll buy you a drink at Blue's."

"Oh, a bet that I'm a part of," Raven said lightheartedly, reaching over to shake the woman's hand.

No one thought she'd be successful, but that was the least of Silas's worries. When everyone got up to start the afternoon portion of the workday, he approached Raven before she could leave the kitchen.

"I need to know your game plan for your meeting with Crawley."

"Well, first, I'll enter his office, then I'll sit down on a chair. If he offers me a drink, I'll decline—"

"Raven."

"Okay, okay. I'm going to ask him to pay what he owes," she said, "and if he doesn't comply... I'll threaten him."

"Fuck it. I'm coming with you."

"I'm not clueless, you know?" she said, her eyebrows slanted in annoyance.

"I know that," he said firmly, hating to have offended her. "I'm not doubting your capabilities, but you don't understand the politics of Cedar Lake. The Crawleys are pandered to because they can make our lives hell."

Raven searched his face for a second then said, "Fine, you can tag along."

So at the end of the day, instead of heading to his truck, Silas got into the passenger seat of Raven's car.

"There's still time to change your mind," he said as he lurched his seat as far back as it would go to give himself more leg room.

"Nope. We're doing this," she said, already reversing out of her spot.

The GPS droned on instructions, and Silas said, "I want you to prepare for this to be a waste of your time."

"Have a little faith. Positive thoughts," she said.

"I know all about positive thinking, but I also like some reality."

"Okay, I once went to this really exclusive club in Miami. The type where if you're not rich or a celebrity, you can't get in. But my friend and I were like, let's give it a shot. Who the fuck knows."

Silas wondered where the hell the story was heading, but he could envision Raven all done up for the club, in a short dress and heels like the different pairs she sometimes wore to work.

"We stood in line," Raven continued, "waiting for like forty minutes, and—"

"Hold up," Silas said. "You waited in line for a club you didn't think you'd get into?"

They'd have to be serving free liquor and possibly have an onsite tax accountant for him to consider it.

"Yes, but let me finish," she said. "When we got to the front of the line with our best smiles, IDs, and a plea for admission, the bouncer let us in with literally no questions. He just lifted the velvet rope."

"And the moral of the story is that it can't hurt to try," he said.

"No, the moral of the story is when people think you're important or someone they're supposed to respect, they tend to."

"I'm lost. How is that the moral?"

"Because before we reached the bouncer, this gorgeous woman and her boyfriend show up, and as they're heading to the front of the line, she drops her liquid lipstick. I see it happen, I pick it up and return it to her, and you'll never guess who she turned out to be…"

Silas sat in dead silence for a few seconds before realizing Raven was pausing for dramatic effect.

"Christ. Who was she, Raven?"

"This celebrity interior designer I only knew because I was working with a realtor at that time who used the designer's book as coffee table decor in her office. I later found out she was dating a Miami Dolphins quarterback. Who also ended up cheating on her with—"

"Is there a point to this story?"

"I'm getting there," she said, lifting her finger to silence him. "We had a brief conversation—like no more than a minute—but it was enough for the bouncer to assume we were acquaintances, that I was somebody."

"And because of that, he let you in," he said.

She nodded. "He let me in."

"Just to make sure I'm clear on your plan then. You're going to pretend to be somebody important with Mr. Crawley?" Silas asked, already stressed at the implication.

"Yeah."

"This is such a bad idea."

"Well, I'm not going to lie and say I'm a princess or something. Google can debunk that easily. But some half truths shouldn't damn my soul."

Silas dropped his face into his hands.

"Relax, we're not pulling off a heist," she said as she turned around a bend before hitting a graveled driveway that delivered them to the Crawley's lakefront log mansion.

"Holy shit," Raven said, leaning forward to get a better view of the home.

"They used to tell us horror stories about this house as kids—how people had gone missing or how bones had been found on the property—so we wouldn't be tempted to trespass."

"Yeah, I can understand children being curious about the castle made out of logs," she said, still gaping at the structure.

At the front entrance, as they waited for the door to be answered, Silas watched Raven rub the small pendant on her necklace. "Is that something special to you? The necklace," he asked.

He'd noticed over the weeks how she'd touch it sometimes mindlessly and at other times like she was talking to it.

"It's a citrine crystal," she said, showing him the amber stone more clearly. "It's for good luck, abundance, joy."

"Oh, okay," he said, leaving his skepticism unsaid. He'd gathered by the way Raven occasionally talked that she held some unconventional beliefs. And hey, they were walking into an unusual situation, so perhaps they needed all the mystical support they could get.

A butler soon welcomed them inside, escorting them quickly through a number of brightly lit hallways with framed art that Silas assumed cost a fortune. They were left in an office with an impressive library and garish furniture, waiting for the boss.

"My friend, Gwen, would love this room," Raven said, studying the ceiling-high bookshelves before quickly pulling out her phone to take pictures.

Meanwhile, Silas was contemplating the kind of gift basket he'd send the Crawleys after the meeting to smooth things over.

When the door to the study opened and Mr. Crawley entered, both he and Raven stood up. As a child, Silas could've sworn the man was at least one hundred years old, but in reality, Mr. Crawley was currently around seventy.

The old man settled in his chair behind the large desk and, perhaps expecting different people, blinked at them before his assistant appeared and whispered something in his ear.

"Oh, yes, Mountaintop Adventures. Great establishment," Mr. Crawley said. "I'm sorry to hear about Charles."

They were empty words. The man didn't care, but Silas graciously nodded.

"You heading it now?" Mr. Crawley asked him.

"No, she is," Silas said easily, gesturing to Raven.

"Hi, I'm Raven."

Her voice had taken up an airier quality than her

natural one, and Silas assumed it was a part of the character she was playing.

"I love your house, by the way," she said. "It's really cute."

The way she said the word "cute" made it seem like the mansion was a quaint little cabin in the woods and not a behemoth of a home with a rumored four-million-dollar price tag. Was this her plan? Give backhanded compliments to persuade the old man to pay his debts?

If Mr. Crawley picked up on the condescension, Silas couldn't tell.

"What can I do for you today, Ms. Raven?"

"I'm obviously new at Mountaintop and Cedar Lake, so I've been going through the books, getting myself familiar with the system and our clients," Raven said. "And I realized we messed up and forgot to charge you for some of the classes and tours you've taken with us in the past."

"Oh?" Mr. Crawley said as his eyes drifted over to Silas, and they seemed to say, "You didn't tell her how things work around here, huh?"

Raven, unaware of the line she was treading, pulled out receipts from a folder she'd been carrying, laying them out one by one in a row on the desk in front of them. It was kind of obscene to see them so blatantly displayed.

Silas hadn't appreciated how much money they'd lost catering to the old man and his family. For the first time since hearing Raven's plans, he was grateful she'd pushed hard to come, even if the mission was ultimately doomed.

Seconds, maybe even minutes, passed before Mr. Crawley said, "Of course. Leave those there. My assistant will take care of it."

Translation: none of those will be paid. But thanks for coming; don't let the door hit you on the way out.

"Fantastic," Raven said, giving herself or Mr. Crawley a little clap.

She thought he'd be sending out that check, and Silas would have to break the news later that there'd be no money coming.

"We appreciate you taking the time from your busy schedule," Raven said, reaching over the desk to offer her hand. "And again, I do really love your house. It reminds me of one of my stepdad's vacation homes."

There it was, the lie she'd cast like a fishing rod.

Silas thought it was too heavy-handed to ring true. And didn't rich people have some type of sonar signal that could detect when other rich people were in their vicinity?

He half expected Mr. Crawley to scream, "Fraud!" and push a button that would plummet him and Raven into the dungeon rumored to exist in the basement.

But the old man's blasé expression shifted slightly. A reassessment.

"Sorry, I didn't ask before, but how did you come to own Mountaintop?" Mr. Crawley asked.

Yes, how did a supposed rich girl come to own a random tour business in a small town?

Raven had seemingly worked out that storyline too, and without taking so much as a breath, she replied, "Charles left me Mountaintop because he dated my mother years ago before she got with my stepfather. And I thought it would be a cool way to prove to myself I can make my own way in the world."

It sounded like a plot to a Lifetime flick, but Silas realized he could bolster her story by displaying some obvious bootlicking to press home the idea that Raven was someone to curry favor with. So he said, "And you're doing an excellent job so far, ma'am."

Raven turned to him, surprise registering briefly in her eyes before she caught on and said, "Thank you, Reynolds," and followed it up with a patronizing pat to his forearm.

"Anyway, we've kept you long enough," Raven said to Mr. Crawley. "We look forward to your future patronage."

Silas was still unconvinced they'd ever see a cent, but at the very least, maybe it would dissuade the wealthy family from using the business as a personal concierge.

They'd almost reached the door when Mr. Crawley called out, "Hold on a second."

In a sequence that Silas could barely believe, they returned to their seats and watched the old man pull out a slim book and make out a check to Mountaintop Adventures for an amount that totaled the unpaid invoices.

Raven had said they weren't pulling off a heist, but as they left the mansion, check in tow, Silas felt adrenaline sweep through him as if it were.

When they entered the quiet confines of Raven's car, Silas said, "Goddamn."

She burst into laughter, and he did too. They found composure eventually, but there was a residual buoyancy.

"I can't believe it worked," he said.

"I told you to have a little faith," she said, pressing her lips to the crystal pendant.

He shrugged. "I guess I was wrong."

She pitched her ear closer to him. "Oh, say that last one again."

"I. Was. Wrong," he repeated, and when she turned to toss him a smug grin, a desire to lean over and kiss her surfaced so abruptly and without cause that he was left speechless.

He straightened in his seat and shook his head like it

might erase the moment, but long after they'd driven away from the affluent premises, Silas couldn't stop thinking, *Where the hell did that come from?*

Chapter Twelve

RAVEN HELD two pairs of earrings up to the side of her face and asked, "Which one?"

"I like the smaller hoops," Gwen said over video call. "But let's back up. You went through that explanation way too quickly. What do you mean you bamboozled some rich guy?"

"The money rightfully belongs to us, first of all," Raven said, searching her suitcase for a particular purse. "Secondly, I didn't *bamboozle* him. I told some half truths— my mom did date a rich guy once, actually. Not filthy rich, but he drove a Lexus and bought Neil Young's guitar pick from an online auction."

Unless Mr. Crawley decided to hire some private investigator that cost more than the invoices he'd paid, Raven couldn't see how he'd find out.

"And you're missing the bigger point here," Raven said to her friend. "The team is starting to sort of accept me."

The morning after obtaining the Crawley's invoice payments, everyone at Mountaintop had been more hype than Raven had expected.

"I'll be honest, I didn't think you could do it, but credit where credit is due," Halo had said, and then they all had agreed on a day they'd get drinks after work.

It had felt like a milestone.

"You're telling me even that Silas guy is cool with you?" Gwen asked.

"I'm still going after something he wants, but yeah, we're cordial now."

For the duration they were in Mr. Crawley's office, they'd felt like partners. He'd trusted her or at least given her enough leeway to take a big swing.

"I'm glad everything seems to be smoothing out for you over there," her friend said. "I was worried I'd have to come and rescue you from that place."

After ending the call with her best friend and settling on a pair of heels, Raven drove to the Blue Dog Bar. There wasn't much to it. It looked like a run-down barn from the outside. Upon entering the packed establishment, she noticed everyone was wearing either denim, flannel, or a combination of both. She stuck out, but no one paid her more than a glance or two as she traversed the bar.

She spotted the team at the back, and as she approached, they all began drumming the table to mimic the thunderous sound of applause.

"Here comes the dragon slayer!" Bodie shouted, and Raven received the attention with a curtsy before slipping onto the stool across from Silas.

Her mouth grew dry when she met his gaze. Under the bar's dim lights, he looked like a portrait painted with confident strokes.

"A deal's a deal," Halo said. "What drink can I get you?"

"My usual is a New York sour," Raven said.

"Okay, hun, this is a glorified dive bar," Halo

explained. "The fanciest drink they'll have is maybe the Silas Reynolds."

Raven turned to look at Silas. "You have a drink named after you?"

He seemed embarrassed, rubbing the back of his neck. "Yeah."

"Why?" she asked.

"He's a town hero. Made it to the 2012 Olympics and brought home the silver in archery," Halo said like it was a well-established fact and not brand-new information to Raven.

"What? Why is this the first time I'm hearing about this?" Raven asked, looking at everyone at the table.

"It's quite literally public information," Silas said.

"No, but why isn't it blazoned on Mountaintop's website?" Raven asked.

"Because it's unnecessary," he said.

Raven hadn't pegged him as overly humble, but maybe he'd somehow lost sight of how amazing his accomplishment was.

"I'm definitely going to get the Silas Reynolds," she told Halo.

"You might not like it," Silas said. "I don't."

"I'm not paying for it, so no skin off my back."

When Halo returned with the drink, Raven took a sip as everyone watched her. It was rum-based, with a lot of syrup—maybe too much—and some pineapple juice, and another flavor she couldn't quite identify.

"What do you think?" Silas asked her.

"You taste good," she said.

———

"It looks like an engagement ring," Halo said.

"Does it?" Bodie asked, studying the picture he'd pulled up on his phone.

The Mountaintop team had paused their pool game to assess the gift Bodie was thinking of getting his girlfriend for her birthday.

"To me, it looks like every ring ever," Doc said.

"If you're worried she's going to think you're proposing, just warn her that you're not beforehand," Silas offered, which evoked a groan from Halo as well as Raven, who held a pool cue in one hand and his eponymous cocktail in the other.

"You taste good," she'd said, describing the drink. He'd nearly fallen off his stool. Even now, her words rang in his head, making Silas feel warm all over.

"That's horrible advice," Raven said to him.

"Why?" Silas asked, enjoying how her lips twisted to emphasize her disgust.

"A caveat like that is tacky," Raven said.

"Okay, but he's getting her a diamond ring, hence the need for a warning," Silas said, drawing nearer and seeing the individual flecks of glitter on Raven's lids.

"Another option is to get her a ring with any of the other dozens of stones," she countered.

Silas cared very little about this debate, but he inexplicably continued, "Maybe she likes diamonds."

"Then he should get her a diamond necklace or bracelet."

"Well, the concept of a diamond engagement ring is fake anyway, invented by—"

"By an ad agency in the forties, yes, yes," she said, with a mocking nod. "But there's a time and place to start breaking decades of conditioning."

He opened his mouth to present another rebuttal, but a

stranger from the edge of the gaming area shouted, "You guys playing or chatting?"

The bar was full tonight, mostly with out-of-town sawmill workers, and the pool tables were in high demand.

"Both, thank you!" Halo shouted back to the stranger.

"I guess we should wrap this up before we get bullied off," Silas said. "Whose turn?"

Doc stepped up. His strategy involved being methodical, so there was zero urgency. He took his time lining up his shot, the tip of his tongue making an appearance. For all that care, Doc still failed to pocket the ball. It was consistent with how he'd done all game.

Similarly, Halo had a poor accuracy rate, but she approached pool with a lot of intensity and power, resulting in many balls jumping off the table.

"Boo!" Halo would shout, but it was unclear if it was directed at herself or the concept of pool in general.

Ultimately, the real competition was between Silas, Bodie, and Raven.

Bodie and Raven had great technique and halfway colluded to eliminate Silas from the game because of his perceived advantage.

"Archery is totally a transferable skill," Raven told him.

Despite his denials, he was shortly eliminated and stood with the other losers to watch Bodie and Raven battle for first.

Raven looked incredible tonight, and Silas had to focus on the trajectory of the balls she struck instead of how her short dress would inch up her thigh when she bent over the table with her cue.

In the days following the moment in Raven's car at the Crawleys', Silas had concluded it was understandable he'd want to kiss a beautiful woman he'd built some rapport with. It didn't mean anything, and it wouldn't go further than his thoughts. It could simply exist as one of the millions of facts about life.

"No!" Raven shouted when Bodie pocketed her final ball, winning the game.

It had grown late, so when the team got back to their table, Halo said, "All right, kids, I've gotta pick up Libby from her friend's."

Doc and Bodie similarly made their exits, and Silas left with Raven once she'd returned from the restroom.

"I'm still hung up on the fact you're a secret Olympian," Raven said as they stepped out of the still-lively bar into the warm evening that smelled of cigarettes and weed.

"There's no secret," he said. "I qualified for 2012 and won two silver medals. I then qualified for Rio but fucked up my arm in an ATV accident a year before and had to drop out."

"Whoa," Raven said, stopping in her tracks, forcing him to as well.

He didn't usually talk about his Olympics journey so transparently. He hated to, in fact. But seeing as Raven appeared curious enough to Google him later, he was trying to fast-track the questions and sympathy he often received afterward.

"I'm so sorry," she said earnestly. "You could've told me to shut up when I was harping on about it all night. I wouldn't have blamed you."

Suddenly needing to allay her embarrassment, he said, "I would have, but we did agree to be cordial and friendly."

She smiled. "We did. And now I'll never bring it up again."

"It's not taboo. It's just a tired topic around here," Silas said as a gust of wind blew the light, wispy ends of Raven's braids into her face. Without thinking, he brushed them away.

It was such an intimate gesture that it froze them both.

During those suspended seconds, tension pulled taut like a rubber band stretched to its limits, and all possibilities—to apologize, to walk away, to shrug—were dismissed for one.

They reached for each other, their lips meeting, and the earth seemed to crack open on contact. A moan sprung from his throat at the feeling of her soft body, her hips shifting toward him.

Their tongues teased as their lips parted, drawing the heat stoking in his body to the surface of his skin. She smelled wonderful, like clean linen dried out in the sun, and he cupped one side of her face to deepen the kiss and somehow capture her essence, intensify it.

He knew he should've pulled away, ended it while he still could play off the moment as trivial. But she pressed close, and he pulled her even closer—sinking into the fevered kisses that tasted faintly of pineapple.

Her fingertips skated across his neck and head before gently closing her hand around his coiled hair. The light tug had his dick agonizingly pressed against the front of his pants.

Physical space stopped meaning much beyond how it facilitated the heated breaths they shared. He'd have stayed there for eternity, nourishing himself only on the lustful sounds that spilled from her beautiful mouth.

But the proverb about all good things coming to an end remained true because a car's obnoxious horn brought the edges of the world back in, ripping them away from bliss.

His body continued to hum as he and Raven stood apart, looking at one other. Her lids were heavy, and her chest dramatically rose and fell; God only knew what she could see in him.

"All right, good night," she said, still breathless, still fucking kissable. The smile she gave him as she turned pinned him in place, and he watched her walk to her car and drive off.

It was several minutes before his hands stopped shaking and he did the same.

Chapter Thirteen

"THE BATHROOM WAS RETILED when the new sink was installed late last year," the realtor, Vivian, said to Raven. "You can see it has the same pinwheel lay pattern the kitchen tiles have."

It was the second house she'd toured that day, and she knew she'd love it when she saw the bright blue front door.

"It's beautiful," Raven said before asking her mom who was on video call, "What do you think?"

"I still can't believe you can afford this," her mom said.

"One of the great things about living in a small town," Vivian replied before a phone from her purse started ringing. She encouraged Raven to take another look around the house as she took the call.

"How many more homes are you looking at today?" her mom asked as they took another turn about the main bedroom.

"One more," Raven said, her words distorted by what felt like her dozenth yawn that hour.

"You didn't get enough sleep or something?" her mom asked.

"Late night," Raven said. "Went to the bar with people from work."

"Oh, how was that?"

"It was fun," Raven said, taking a sudden interest in the stone that made up the fireplace area.

"Uh-oh. What happened?" her mom asked.

"Nothing. I said it was fun."

"You would have gone into detail already if it were fun."

For a moment, Raven debated sticking to her vague assertion, not wanting to make a big deal of what had kept her up most of the night, but the next words out of her mouth were "I made out with someone I probably shouldn't have."

"Is he married?" her mom asked without missing a beat.

"No."

"A musician?"

"God, no."

"Baby, don't tell me he's a politician."

"Mom, it was Silas."

"Oh. Wow, okay. Did not expect that."

"It was great, honestly," Raven said. "Usually I think of first kisses as being meh or complete disasters. But this one was so confident with literally zero awkwardness. I'd crown it the best I've ever experienced."

Raven realized after she stopped speaking that her comments sounded too enthusiastic.

"You don't like him, right?" her mom asked, her face turning serious. "I don't want you getting caught up."

"No, no," Raven said, laughing lightly. "Please. It was something that happened in front of a dive bar."

But Raven and her mom both knew how Raven tended to lose her head when she got infatuated. Her common sense got pixelated, and she'd jump into relationships that burned bright and hot but eventually fizzled out.

However, this situation was completely different.

The excitement she was feeling could be mostly assigned to the ego boost the make-out gave her. She'd been feeling pathetic for lusting over Silas, so it felt good to know the attraction wasn't one-sided. That was all.

"I know why I'm here," Raven said to her mom. "You don't have to worry."

———

"The band has a gig coming up," Doc said to the Mountaintop team as they walked into the break room first thing in the morning. "Let me know if you're interested, and I'll reserve tickets for you."

"You bet your ass I'm interested," Halo said.

"We doing a carpool again?" Bodie asked as he placed Chestnut in his playpen. "If so, Tess wants to come."

"I'm cool with picking everyone up and being DD," Silas said.

"Great," Doc replied. "And I'm also inviting Raven, just so everyone knows."

The team turned to Silas. For a second, he thought they'd somehow found out about his kiss with Raven over the weekend, but it turned out they were simply wondering if he'd contest Doc's arrangement.

"Guys, we've been over this. I'm okay with Raven joining us for things we do as a group," Silas said before starting his coffee over at the counter.

Silas had decided he wouldn't bring up the kiss unless Raven did. It had been a mistake. How was he supposed to conduct himself with some level of professionalism when he was recalling her curves or the weight of her arms on his shoulders? What made things worse was now he knew she was attracted to him too, and he was a little bothered by the dopamine hit he got every time he thought about that.

"Morning, everyone," Raven said cheerfully, entering the break room as if summoned by his thoughts.

Her sudden appearance had Silas knocking over the box of coffee filters, but Raven was briefly pulled into a conversation happening at the table, giving Silas a moment to compose himself.

She eventually made her way to the counter space beside him, where she began making her morning beverage.

"Hey," he said, casting her a look as he dumped sugar and creamer into his cup.

She smiled, meeting his eye. "Hi."

It felt like looking directly into the sun.

The kiss seemingly had no noteworthy impact on Raven because she was cool and at ease next to him. Meanwhile, Silas was worried he was breathing too hard.

He found his place at the table, Raven followed shortly after, and conversation floated past Silas as he considered what he should do. He could not continue to feel unmoored over a kiss. It was ridiculous.

He'd been too flirtatious at the bar. He'd gotten comfortable, so the kiss had been an easy, perhaps inevitable, progression. Maybe he needed to bring back some stringency from their earlier interactions. Basic politeness only.

He took a mouthful of his coffee but immediately spat what he'd imbibed back into the mug.

"Fuck," he shouted, bitterness and brine coating his tongue.

Everyone turned to him with a mix of horror and concern.

"What's wrong?" Halo asked.

"I added salt, not sugar," he managed to say as he grabbed his water bottle to rinse his mouth.

The entire team found his flub amusing, slapping the table and cackling loudly, but it was the way Raven laughed behind her hand that made him, for the smallest discernible unit of time, consider slapstick comedy.

Yeah, it would be total politeness from here on out.

———

A day of interactions between Raven and Silas went as follows: a regular greeting in the morning, small talk during lunch, brief goodbyes at the end of the day, and most importantly, absolutely no references to the Kiss.

It appeared they'd both independently come to the same conclusion that the kiss had been ill-advised and would never happen again.

All the lighthearted energy they'd cultivated between them was gone. There was none of the strain or irritation of her early days at Mountaintop, just blandness. Which Raven convinced herself was fine. She was in Cedar Lake for a bigger purpose than to engage in banter with a man, after all.

That's not to say she'd reached nonchalance in regard to Silas. Because when Doc in the middle of the week said, "Raven, you're on the schedule to shadow Silas's archery class today," she immediately wanted to cancel.

However, it would've required Raven to admit that the kiss had meant something, so she attended the class.

Right off the bat, when Silas welcomed her and the

seven other students to his archery introductory, his strong and resonant voice raised goose bumps across her arms.

"If you take any lesson from today," Silas said after going over safety and the gear, "let it be that you should never pull on an empty bowstring. It'll damage the bow or, worse, injure you. That wouldn't be good because I skipped the last day of first aid training."

Despite his occasional jokes, Silas fostered a serious learning environment that made Raven feel like she was practicing for mastery. She carefully listened and watched Silas demonstrate basic archery form and the steps involved in shooting.

After bows and quivers full of arrows were distributed, it was time for Raven and the other students to combine all his pithy instructions and attempt to hit ringed targets a distance away. Raven immediately found the equipment clumsy and bulky in her hands, and her arrows failed to go in any consistent direction.

Silas was going around to everyone and providing specific and personalized instruction, and when he finally approached Raven, she'd yet to make any real progress with accuracy.

"Let's see what you got," he said to her.

Quelling the flutter in her stomach, Raven got in position, lifting her bow and pulling the string back.

"Rotate your elbow away from the bow," he said, giving her something to do rather than focus on how his dark eyes tracked her movements.

"Too much," he said, and with the lightest touch, almost phantasmal, he adjusted her arm.

"Now what?" she asked, her voice raspier than she'd have liked.

"Draw and release," he instructed.

She pulled the string back until her thumb touched the

corner of her mouth as he'd shown them, and she let the bowstring slip past her fingers. The arrow flew through the air, landing several feet to the left of its intended mark. It was the best shot she'd taken in the entire class.

"Good," he said with a polite smile that still managed to do something to her. "Try again, but now drop your shoulders."

She nocked another arrow, aimed at the target, pulled the string, adjusted her shoulders, and released.

The shot was better, but still off the mark.

"You hold your breath at full draw," he said, picking up his recurve bow. "Don't forget to breathe."

With exaggerated inhales and exhales, he showed her how he paired his breath with each movement, and she was transfixed by how fluidly he moved. The muscles in his shoulders and chest bulged as he lifted his bow and drew the bowstring across his wide body. When the arrow left his bow and whizzed through the air, it landed dead center on the target ahead.

"Make sense?" he asked, turning his eyes on her, and all she could manage was a nod.

He moved on to the next student then, and she was left feeling discombobulated and tense in a weird and unspecific way. All Raven knew was she might've spoken too soon when she told her mother she had nothing to worry about.

Chapter Fourteen

AT THE CRACK OF DAWN, Silas received a text from his brother: *Things have gone to shit. Come over ASAP.*

Of course, Silas panicked and called Isaiah while he was shoving his legs into a pair of jeans. But his brother clarified over the phone, "It's not an end-of-the-word sort of thing. Take a shower, eat breakfast, then come over."

Silas deduced that something had gone wrong with Maggie and Leon's birthday party planning, which was not ideal, seeing as the party was that very afternoon.

When he arrived at his brother's home, he found Victor alone in the kitchen furiously mixing ingredients in a bowl while a baking instructional video played on an iPad perched on top of a row of mason jars.

"What happened?" Silas asked.

His brother-in-law stopped long enough to say, "The dogs got into the cake and decorations in the middle of the night. Isaiah dropped off the kids at their friend's so we can concentrate on salvaging the party before noon."

Silas put down the presents he'd come along with. "What can I do?"

"There are leftover toys and candy in the dining room, so if you could remake as many party favor bags as possible, that'd be great," Victor said. "Then you can take the tables to the yard and start setting those up, and if you finish that, you can figure out how to use the popcorn machine."

"I'm on it," Silas said, not thinking too hard about whether the list was accomplishable in the time frame.

He situated himself in the dining room in a one-man assembly line, making decent headway by the time his brother showed up an hour later with shopping in hand and despondency all over his face.

"There were no more yellow balloons, so I got green and red balloons. Our circus theme has officially turned into a Christmas celebration," Isaiah said.

"No one is going to think Christmas when they see that photo board cutout with the contortionist and clown."

His brother nodded, briefly mollified, until his husband shouted from the other room, "Fuck!"

Victor entered the dining room clutching his phone. "Want more bad news?"

"Not if you can help it," Isaiah said.

"The bouncy castle rental company can't deliver," Victor said. "Apparently their van has a flat tire, and since they're driving over from the next county, they can't fix it and make it on time."

"Murphy's Law is really in charge today, huh?" Isaiah said wryly, moments before the air around them turned acrid.

"Is something burning?" Silas asked, shooting to his feet.

"Dammit," Victor said, rushing back into the kitchen only to return with a tray of blackened cupcakes.

"This is a disaster," Silas's brother said with a laugh tinged with hysteria.

"You know what? Forget the decorations, forget the cake. It's a party for first-graders," Victor said with a defeatist shrug. "Fae is still coming with the catering—knock on wood—and we can put on some music and pick up some ice cream. It'll be fine."

"And there's still your special guest," Isaiah added.

"Exactly. We've tried and obviously failed. There's always next year," Victor said.

"Wait, no," Silas said, looking between the husbands. "What happened to the hippocampus developing and creating a moment to remember?"

"There's not enough time to pull this off," Victor said, already removing the apron around his waist.

"Like hell there's not. Where's your planner?" Silas asked.

Victor hesitated but handed Silas a notepad with a to-do list.

"Okay, good. This is manageable," Silas said, mentally dividing the tasks.

"What?" his brother said. "How?"

"Don't worry about it. You two just focus on finishing baking. I'll deal with the rest."

Isaiah and Victor both skeptically looked at him, but with nothing to lose by giving him a chance to pull this party off, they left for the kitchen to crank out some cupcakes.

Meanwhile, Silas texted the Mountaintop team group chat, recruiting help from anyone who could spare the time. He offered food in exchange.

Within thirty minutes, Doc, Bodie, and Halo had shown up. It was so good to see his motley crew.

"I love you guys," Silas said to them as he set them up with different tasks.

"This isn't for you. It's for the lunch you promised," Halo said with a wink before she picked up where he'd left off with the party favor bags.

"Do you want the napkins folded horizontally or vertically?" Bodie asked him from a place at the dining table.

Silas looked at the square napkins. "Your choice, man."

Doc came in grinning, holding a bicycle pump he'd found in the garage. "It'll make blowing up the balloons more efficient," he said.

"If there was any doubt you were a resourceful genius," Halo said in amazement.

Confident everything was being executed smoothly, Silas left for the backyard and quickly set up the food tables and figured out how to operate the popcorn machine. When he entered the kitchen, dozens of cupcakes were cooling on every available surface.

"Can you help with cakes, so I can do the dishes before they get out of hand?" Isaiah said. "Victor's gone to get the special guest."

"Okay, can you please tell me who this special guest is?"

"Come on, it's not obvious?" Isaiah asked. "You didn't notice Victor was wearing a wig cap the entire time?"

"Oh, wait, is it Miss Olivia Justice?" Silas asked, but of course it was, and the kids would certainly lose their minds when the drag queen appeared.

With a couple of hours until the party was supposed to start, Silas worked quickly, covering the cupcakes in store-bought buttercream.

"Raven hasn't shown up yet?" Isaiah said after a while.

"No, she got the text, though. But at this point, we

don't need her help," Silas said casually, but if he were truthful, he'd admit he was relieved she hadn't come. The last week of interactions between him and Raven had amounted to a series of stilted sentences after another. He didn't need that on a day like today.

The doorbell rang, and Isaiah abandoned his place at the sink to answer it. Silas barely registered his brother's departure until he heard her voice.

Moments later, Raven and his brother entered the kitchen, laughing and talking like they were old friends. Silas watched them, frozen.

"What can I do?" Raven asked Isaiah.

"Depends. How do you feel about sprinkles?"

"Positively," Raven said.

"Then you can wash your hands and be on sprinkle duty next to Silas."

She finally looked over at Silas, and he barely had time to mentally adjust to her sudden arrival before they were sharing elbow space. Isaiah left to check up on the catering while Silas and Raven worked to find a rhythm decorating together.

"The cupcakes smell good," she said.

"Brown sugar maple," he replied.

Their fingers brushed, their shoulders bumped, and each time Raven moved to set aside a platter of fully completed cupcakes, she would lightly press her hand to the center of his back as she passed behind him.

They were brief contacts that didn't mean anything, but in accumulation, they left him feeling like he was floating.

Soon the house started to grow loud. People were coming in and out of the kitchen, bursting the little bubble that had formed around the two of them.

His niece and nephew ran into the kitchen, dressed and ready for their sixth birthday celebration.

"Uncle Silas!" they called out. He gathered the two in his arms, lifting his nephew—the lighter of the two—in his weaker arm.

"Looking fresh, lil' man," Silas said to the boy. "Mags, you look beautiful as always."

"Zander got into the decorations and cake," Maggie told him, her Fulani braids hitting him in the face as she animatedly spoke.

"I heard, but we're taking care of it, so no need to worry at all," he said, placing them back on their feet.

"Who's that?" Leon asked in what could barely be considered a whisper as he stealthily pointed to Raven.

"Hi, hi, happy birthday," Raven said, putting down the cupcakes to address the kids. "I'm Raven, the friendly sprinkle expert. It's nice to meet you."

She gave them both solid handshakes like they were equals, and Silas watched as the twins straightened their tiny shoulders as if to merit the respect Raven was showing them.

"I like your dress," Leon said, dragging his fingers over the frilly fabric of her sleeve.

"Thank you. I think you both look real spiffy," Raven responded.

"Spiffy?" Maggie said, placing her hand on her hip. "What's that mean?"

"It means you look good," Raven said.

Maggie nodded and said the word quietly as if committing it to memory while Leon peeked over at the counter and said, "The cupcakes look really spiffy."

Raven laughed joyously, and the moment needled a place in Silas's brain.

———

The birthday party was in full swing. The adults mingled in the living room while the kids were squealing and gorging on cupcakes in the backyard.

Raven had been introduced to more townspeople today than in the last weeks. Many of them responded with an "Oh, *you're* Raven" after meeting her.

Then she'd get some version of "How're you liking Cedar?"

"I'm loving it," she'd say. "Still haven't gone down to the lake, but I see it every time I drive to work."

Raven managed to slip away from a conversation with a small group of parents discussing a new school policy in order to search the catering table for more fried plantain. But as she feared, they'd been completely devoured.

Hope was renewed, however, when Bodie appeared beside her and revealed a plate of them that he'd covered with a napkin and whispered, "There's more in the kitchen."

"You are amazing," she told him before making a beeline to the kitchen. When she found Isaiah at the sink doing the dishes, she felt uncomfortable demanding the location of the plantain.

Isaiah noticed her and nodded toward the scene on the other side of the window. "I can't tell who's having more fun, Miss Olivia Justice, Silas, or the kids."

Raven joined him to look out into the backyard. Isaiah's partner and Silas led the kids in a series of basic carnival games.

"It just might be a tie," Raven finally said.

She had never seen Silas so animated and goofy. He contorted his features to the amusement of the kids, putting in the effort needed to stand toe-to-toe with Miss

Olivia Justice, who was naturally enthralling with her giant pink afro and flouncy skirt.

Raven laughed watching Silas fall and stumble during a demo of a game that required he spin in a circle several times.

When she found Isaiah studying her, she muted her expression, concerned with what he might find otherwise. "How did you and Victor meet?" she asked to avoid further scrutiny.

Isaiah's face softened. "He was some burnt-out lawyer who'd escaped to the mountains to relax and maybe write a novel. I was in a rush and bumped into him as I was leaving the clinic. It felt like Cupid struck me right then and there."

"Sounds serendipitous," Raven said as a sudden yearning surfaced, pressing against her sternum.

She was no stranger to the kind of instantaneous connection Isaiah described, but her relationships had never had the staying power that Isaiah and Victor's clearly had.

As the afternoon progressed, more games were played, more cake was consumed, and an energetic rendition of "Happy Birthday" was sung/shouted. And when the party officially ended, parents and kids with grass-stained clothes left the house with smiles on their faces.

Raven hung back with the rest of the Mountaintop group to help clean, but Isaiah chased them out too, saying, "Please, go! You've done more than enough for us today!"

In the driveway, Silas thanked them. "I appreciate you guys."

"Of course," Halo said as she hugged him. "See you Monday."

They all splintered off toward their vehicles they'd

parked in different areas in the neighborhood. Raven and Silas realized they were headed in the same direction and fell into step with one another.

"I didn't realize you were such a dork," Raven said to him after a moment, and his hearty laugh traveled through the quiet street.

"I had to embrace it when I became an uncle," he said.

"I'm sure they appreciate it," Raven said. "Also, it was a great party."

"Yeah," Silas agreed. "If I hadn't been in the thick of things, I wouldn't have known it was a near-disaster."

"As long as there's enthusiasm and some music, it's hard to make a party a complete disaster," Raven said.

"Ah, you weren't there for my eleventh birthday party at the bowling alley," Silas said. "I broke my big toe two days before and couldn't wear the bowling shoes. It was too late to cancel, so I spent my own party watching my friends bowl."

"No," Raven said sympathetically as she struggled not to laugh at the visual he painted.

"Oh, you think it's funny?" he asked, turning to her in feigned annoyance. They had stopped at the midpoint between their vehicles.

"Of course not," she said, placing her hand on his bicep as if truly concerned.

Silas's gaze dipped to where she touched him, and Raven, realizing her mistake, snatched her hand away.

They were still in a precarious place after their kiss. She could keenly recall the moment-by-moment sensations she'd experienced in his arms, and as she met his dark, smoldering gaze, she knew she wanted nothing more than to feel his lips press against hers again.

She could feel his body heat and see the expansion of his chest with each breath he took. It seemed like they were drawing closer and she'd get her wish, but before the moment could coalesce into something satisfying, Silas said, "Good night, Raven."

They parted ways, and Raven sat in her car for a while, the thumping of her heart filling her ears.

Chapter Fifteen

SILAS HAD NEARLY MADE it to the kitchen during his midmorning break when Raven, from behind the front desk, called him over.

He'd almost kissed her again days ago in the middle of his brother's neighborhood, of all places. He'd momentarily forgotten his commitment to absolute politeness while studying her under the soft glow of the streetlights. Her lips had been parted, her breathing shallow, and he'd known she'd wanted to kiss him too.

But he'd done the levelheaded thing, the difficult thing, and walked away. God only knew where he'd found the strength.

"Do you have time to talk?" she asked when he reached her work area.

Her braids were styled into a low bun, and the dress she wore, he supposed, might've looked casual if it weren't for the pile of gold jewelry on her wrists.

"I have an introductory class in thirty," he said.

"Okay, I'll make it quick," she said, joining him on the other side of the desk with a file. "Since you know Cedar

Lake better than I do, I wanted your thoughts on my ideas for Mountaintop."

A business consultation.

Silas experienced a mix of emotions. Her request was a reminder that Mountaintop was not his. But it was also validating that Raven was interested in his perspective.

"What do you think about partnership marketing with a hotel or motel in town?" she asked, opening the file detailing her plan. "I know that, for instance, the rodeo does something similar to great results."

Silas scanned the documents. "So it would be a long-term referral partnership? We'd have to pick the right hotel to fit our brand."

"Yeah, and maybe we can develop a program that benefits us both," she said, stepping closer to flip the page. "I once worked closely with a product manager for this start-up that made watches, and they collaborated with a marathon organizer to design a special watch for a major race."

"It sounds like a really good idea to me," he said, feeling a thread of excitement over the potential of her plan.

"Awesome, thanks for your help," Raven said, and as she returned the papers to her file, she asked, "How's your morning been so far?"

"Good. Nothing unusual," he said. "You?"

"I knocked out a few admin tasks," she said. "Also had some guy come in who was convinced this was a shooting range. Claimed Google told him it was here. Then got testy when I showed him otherwise."

She laughed, but Silas tensed.

"Do you get people coming in here getting rude with you?" he asked carefully.

The question seemed to surprise Raven, but she waved

her hand and said, "Oh, rarely ever. And it's never anything I haven't seen before."

"You know if anyone is giving you a hard time, you can call me over on the walkie-talkie," he said, still disturbed by the thought of her confronting angry clients. "Not insinuating that you can't handle yourself, obviously."

"Sweet offer, but honestly, it's not necessary," she said before chuckling. "I just pictured you shooting an arrow from all the way in the field and pinning a rude customer by their shirt like a cartoon character."

She looked so beautiful when she laughed.

"I don't know if I'm that good," he said with a smile.

As their mirth faded, silence took its place. He thought of leaving for the break room but felt anchored to that spot. She didn't move either, and the longer they remained still, the more convinced Silas was that they'd never leave. But then Raven's eyes fluttered to his mouth, and the next breath they took was while their bodies converged.

His hands circled her waist while her arms flung around his shoulders. When their lips met, a vibration, starting in his spine, took hold of him. With awkward steps, they landed against a wall in the cabin, and he maneuvered them until they were inside the supply closet.

He pressed her against the door, and her hand settled behind his head, pulling him deeper into the kiss. Her tongue, soft and hot, fueled him, and he palmed her lush thighs and ass over the light material of her dress.

Any hope he had of stopping the progression of the kiss ended the moment Raven started moving her hips in a circle. When a moan left her mouth, it filtered through him straight to his dick.

He pressed his lips against her chin, working his way to the hollow of her neck, feeling the tiny shivers pulsing off her body.

"You smell so fucking good," he whispered while peppering kisses across the swell of her breasts that her outfit exposed.

Finding the hem of her dress, Silas dragged his hand up her bare leg. He'd made it to Raven's upper thigh when in a breathy, faraway voice, she said, "Silas."

A responding sound emerged from his throat, hearing her say his name like that.

"No, Silas," she said, slapping his shoulder. "Someone's in the office."

He stilled and listened past their heavy breathing. And just like she said, they were no longer alone in the cabin.

Stepping away from Raven felt like being thrown into frigid water. He wanted her heat back. While she fixed her dress and her makeup, he halfheartedly straightened the shirt she'd rumpled.

"Who leaves first?" he asked, his voice like sandpaper even to his own ears.

"Me," she said, then pointed to the obvious bulge at the front of his pants. "You need to wait that out."

"Yes, ma'am," he said before she left him alone in the closet.

He leaned over one of the shelves, knowing he'd just tossed himself into the deep end with that kiss.

———

Raven spent her weekends in Cedar Lake as leisurely as possible. She went to the small farmers' market in town and did long beauty routines inside her motel room. But today, she couldn't stand to be in her own company and sought out Linda to ask her what she could do in Cedar for fun.

"You could go to Blue's," the older woman had said.

"Or Crestwood Park. You can go hiking or biking. Oh, we have a few boutiques that might interest you."

No doubt, her less-than-enthused expression prompted Linda to say, "I have a book club meeting today if you want to join us."

That's how Raven ended up sitting on a foldable chair in front of the motel's outdoor pool with a group of eight women who called themselves the Beach Readers. It was the sort of collection of people Raven imagined a small town's website would love to feature to combat stereotypes. Ethnically diverse people congregate here, see!

Raven thought she'd have to nod and listen as the women discussed an unfamiliar novel, but while there were books present, Raven discovered the Beach Readers was more of a group therapy session where advice was dispensed.

For instance, Mellie shared her anxieties about leaving a job she'd held since she was in her twenties, nervous about breaking the news to her longtime boss. The Readers helped her write out and practice her resignation speech.

Jan fretted about her son not wanting to go to college, positive stand-up comedy was not the path for him.

The group helped her reason with her fears.

"Look at what's-his-face, the bald comedian on that sketch show. He grew up in a small town in the States," Hannah said.

"Isn't he the one who was charged recently for fraud?" Chioma asked.

"Oh, yeah, that was him," Hannah said pensively. "I think it was a crypto phishing scam."

Before Jan's face could completely drop in defeat, Raven offered, "But your son, Jan, could be funny and successful without committing federal offenses."

The group agreed.

The meeting turned out to be the perfect distraction for Raven and her bustling mind. That is, until Kriti asked her, "Okay, what's your dilemma?"

"What?" Raven asked, looking around to find the Readers were now focused on her. "Oh, I have nothing."

"You can't attend and not share something," Linda said, and Raven wished she'd been informed of that rule before showing up.

"It doesn't have to be a big, dark secret," one of the women insisted.

"Okay, then," Raven said. "I need help picking my nail polish color for the new week. I was thinking either a canary yellow or an olive."

"The problem has to be a little meatier than that, sweetie," Linda said.

Raven scanned the earnest faces in the group, realizing she might get useful advice for her most pressing crisis. "I have a crush on someone, and I need to get over it as quickly as possible."

It sounded pitiful out loud, but the women nodded understandingly.

"Is it someone in Cedar?" Linda asked, and Raven discerned a slight forward shift everyone made in their seats.

"Oh, no," Raven quickly said. She would rather dive headfirst into the shallow pool than name Silas. "He's from back home. A friend of a friend."

And Raven was glad that no one pressed for further details as they grew silent to ponder a solution.

She was in unfamiliar territory. Her crushes had never been this high stakes, so she couldn't pursue the connection like she usually might. Regardless of how much she wanted to experience a kiss like the one in the closet again.

"You only have three options, in my opinion," Danika said, assigning each point a finger. "Get over it by—you know—getting under someone else."

There was a scattering of agreement and approval at that suggestion.

But Raven would not be attempting that in a small town. She'd end up screwing the guy who handled the salad bar at the grocery store, which seemed like an unnecessary awkwardness to deal with whenever she wanted a garden salad.

"You can also stifle it," Danika continued. "Crushes are fleeting. If not fed, they tend to wither away."

Raven nodded. It was true. But unfortunately, that would be a little harder for her since she worked with Silas and saw him almost daily. And if she decided to stay, she'd have to figure out how to manage it.

"What's the last one?" Raven asked.

"Embrace it," Danika said, and Raven wanted to scream.

She thanked the woman, knowing she was nowhere closer to figuring out how to handle her predicament.

———

The moment Silas opened the door to his brother's vet clinic, a black lab lumbered toward him and immediately exposed his belly. Silas also didn't hesitate to bend to give the good boy a rub.

"Levi, for the love of God, you're giving people the impression I never pet you," said Ms. Edie, an old Black woman whose razor-sharp tongue was notorious across town.

Silas greeted the older woman, and she paused to

assess him and his brother, who'd followed her out of the patient room.

"It's a wonder how your parents didn't go broke feeding you boys," Ms. Edie said.

"Maybe that's why they were so reluctant to retire," Isaiah said.

"They still on vacation? When are they coming back?" Ms. Edie asked as she handed Silas Levi's leash to attach.

"Mid-September," Isaiah said.

"So they'll be back in time for the first snowfall, ha! Foul decision," she said before patting Isaiah and saying, "Okay, I'm off. Thank you for seeing Levi last minute, Dr. Reynolds."

"It's not a problem, ma'am."

"Say hi to that husband of yours for me."

Silas gave the Labrador a few more scratches before letting him follow his owner out the door.

Isaiah turned off the open sign, locked the door, then asked, "Remind me what you came to pick up."

"Calcium block for Chestnut, the squirrel," Silas said.

"Right, yes," his brother said, leading him into an office that had belonged to their father before he'd retired. Isaiah was the spitting image of him in his lab coat.

"Catch," his brother said as he tossed the packaged item to Silas.

"Thanks, man," Silas said.

"How's lemonade-making?" his brother asked, taking a seat on the edge of the office table.

"Huh?"

"You know, that whole situation with Mountaintop and Raven that you're trying to make the best of," Isaiah said.

"Oh, yeah, it's fine. It's going along," Silas said with a shrug.

"Need details. Is she closer to making a decision? Has she implemented any weird rules?"

"No, and no, but I did make out with her twice," Silas said, surprising himself and his brother.

There was silence, then laughter from Isaiah. Real hearty, exuberant laughter that went on and on.

"Why are you laughing?" Silas asked, frowning.

"Listen, your love life has been boring. Nothing worth talking about," Isaiah said, catching his breath. "You're a straight athlete who's always gotten the girl. Yawn. This though? Sleeping with the enemy? That's some drama. It's giving Tyler Perry Presents."

"Now, who said anything about sex? Also, fuck you."

"You have to explain how this happened," his brother said.

"It was a heat-of-the-moment thing," Silas said, rubbing his face.

His strictly polite approach had failed miserably. For the whole week following their moment in the storage closet, Silas had adopted a strategy he called *avoid, avoid, avoid*.

"You in love with her?" his brother asked.

"Man, what? No. Why the fuck would you ask that?"

"Because if it were benign, you wouldn't have even mentioned it. You wouldn't be so... panicky."

"If she were any other woman, it wouldn't matter. But the kiss complicates an already complicated situation," Silas said.

There was a common refrain in archery about how archers can't shoot what they don't look at, and Silas had found that to be the case in life too. He'd lost his entire career because he couldn't keep his eye on the prize.

"I need to focus, and I'm not focusing," Silas said to his brother. "And I don't need her thinking I somehow gave up my dream of owning Mountaintop because I like kissing her."

"The solution is obvious, no?" his brother said.

"I promise if it were, I wouldn't still be standing here," Silas replied.

"Talk to her. Say what you just said to me, to Raven."

It was a simple answer. Maybe the correct one. They had never addressed their attraction—it was the elephant in the room they'd been conveniently sidestepping. Perhaps acknowledging the make-outs would lessen their power and clear the fog obscuring their opposing goals.

Chapter Sixteen

"THE FACT of the matter is he breached our telepathic agreement," Raven said to her best friend on a call over speakerphone.

The friends were at opposite stages of their nights. Gwen had just returned from her mother's retirement dinner, and Raven was preparing to leave for Doc's concert.

She was perched on top of her motel bathroom counter, applying lash strips as she detailed her frustrations with Silas and their two make-out sessions.

"I'm still stuck on how you went all TV medical drama and hooked up with him at work."

"Listen. It was so fucking hot, but I don't want the lines to get blurry," Raven said.

She was already having trouble figuring out how to behave around him.

"You need to have a clear and honest conversation to keep it professional then," Gwen said. "Recommit to those boundaries."

Raven groaned. It was a more reasonable solution than

what the Beach Readers had given her, but it would require a conversation she didn't know how to broach.

"Okay, enough about Silas. Tonight, I'm going to drink, I'm going to dance, and if anyone catches my eye, I'm going to go with it."

The friends' call ended shortly after that, and the next notification from her phone was a text from Bodie letting her know the carpool had arrived. She stepped out of her motel into the dusky evening and spotted Silas's parked truck when he flashed his headlights.

"Excited for tonight?" Raven asked everyone as she hopped into the back of the vehicle, joining Bodie and his girlfriend, Tess.

"So excited!" Tess replied with a small clap while Bodie did a slo-mo head bang and stuck out his tongue.

"My daughter is at my mother's, and I've taken a nap and an antacid. I'm ready," Halo said from her place in the passenger seat. Raven's eyes then briefly met Silas's in the rearview mirror, and a tingling sensation skated across her skin.

He asked, "Good to go?" to which she nodded and fastened her seatbelt. Light conversation circulated throughout the hour-long journey. When they arrived at their destination, the sky was totally dark and the venue was packed. They were forced to park at an odd angle close to an embankment.

"Thank God for four-wheel drive," Halo said as they hopped out of the truck. Together, dressed as if attending different concerts, they walked into the small building.

"Doc!" they all shouted when they saw their friend waiting for them near the doors with their tickets. He looked bashful as they approached and showered him with hugs and excitement. He'd lined his eyes with dark liner and messily slicked back his hair.

"I can't wait to hear you guys live," Raven said.

She'd redone their website, and in the process had listened to their music. A lot of Desktopia's songs off their EP had mellow verses that built into shouty, emotional choruses.

"I probably won't get to see you after the show," Doc said. "But thanks for coming."

When they were let into the actual concert area with stamps on their hands, it was full of people milling around waiting for things to start.

"First round of shots on me," Raven said to the group, raising her voice to be heard over the din.

"Need help?" Silas asked her.

"Sure," she answered automatically but regretted it right away.

While they waited their turn at the small bar at the back, she thought maybe this would be the time to bring up the kiss and set some boundaries, but she quickly realized the space was too loud to have any meaningful conversation. Instead, to mitigate awkwardness, she asked, "How many of Doc's gigs have you attended?"

She had to lean in for him to hear her, and he similarly had to when he responded, "Five or six?"

His warm breath coasted over her ear and neck, and if she pressed a little closer, she would feel his beard against her cheek.

"What kind of music do you listen to?" he asked her.

"I'm more of a top-forty pop and R&B girl, but I'll listen to anything," she said. "You?"

"Hip-hop, mostly, but also country music is unavoidable in Cedar."

Thankfully their uninspired conversation concluded when the bartender shouted for their order, and they soon returned to the group and doled out the drinks.

"To a fun night and to Doc," Raven said before they tossed their shots back. The warm liquid flowed through her body as the lights dimmed, and a heavy strum of an electric guitar reverberated through the room.

"We're Desktopia. And this is for the lost, the searching, and the heartbroken," the front man shouted before the drummer hit her sticks together for a four count and a wall of sound launched from the speakers.

In that moment, Raven was grateful that if nothing could solve her problems, she could at least temporarily forget them and dance.

————

Silas always loved attending Doc's concerts. Mainly because he felt proud—like a big brother—watching Doc and his band rouse audiences to move and surrender to the music.

Everyone was enjoying themselves. Bodie wrapped his arms around Tess from behind, and the two danced in tandem. Halo, who was already somewhere between tipsy and drunk, swayed more or less to the beat. But it was Raven who had him wishing the club soda in his hand was something stronger.

He'd been going on and on to his brother about focusing, but here he was splitting his time between the artists on stage and Raven. In his defense, it was hard not to watch her. She moved her hips and arms to the driving percussion, completely absorbed, and it was, simply put, sexy.

"Where do we go from here?" sang the front man with all the angst the breakup song needed, and Silas challenged himself not to look Raven's way until the end of the song. When he made it, he amended his goal and tried to remain engaged with the performance all the way through the second chorus of the new song. Unfortunately, he didn't meet this target and was pummeled by the sight of Raven with a man.

Silas couldn't make out much of the guy in the dark room, but Raven and his face were inches apart. The guy also had his arms around Raven's waist, damn near cradling her ass.

A nasty twist in Silas's stomach made him tear his gaze away, and it was just the thing to ensure he wouldn't cast another look Raven's way for the rest of the night.

Songs came and went, some original, others covers, and the band progressively got sweatier and unrestrained, and the audience danced and shouted to match their energy. When the group finally hit the last note in their set, they earned the cheers from the crowd. Silas felt some guilt whistling and hollering for Doc and his bandmates as they left the stage, knowing the music had been glorified background noise to his rolling thoughts.

The lights in the room turned on without warning, exposing the blinking and sweat-slick faces of the satisfied attendees. Everyone moved en masse toward the exit, and with a plan already in place for the team to meet at the door, Silas went with the flow of bodies until he was standing in the night air. He flagged down the others as he spotted them.

Raven was the last of their group to emerge from the building, and she was with the man she'd been dancing with inside. Again there was a twist in his stomach watching them hug and hearing an exuberant laugh tumble out of her. When she finally joined the Mountaintop crew, she said, "Sorry for making you wait."

They trudged as a group to Silas's truck, and once he'd set up Halo in the passenger seat with a plastic bag and made sure everyone was buckled in, he pulled out of the venue's parking lot.

When he hit a stretch of uncongested road, he opened a few windows, letting a comfortable breeze filter in. Halo remained bent over the bag in her lap, Bodie and Tess dozed off against one another, and Raven appeared lost in thought as she looked out at the passing scenery.

If Silas were sure the others wouldn't hear him, this moment would be the perfect time to broach a conversation with Raven about their unspoken attraction. But, alas, he'd have to postpone the talk for another day.

The quiet roads helped them arrive in Cedar faster, and Raven was the first person Silas dropped off. As she was closing the door, she said to him, "Thanks for the ride and for being DD."

He watched her enter her room before driving ten minutes to Tess and Bodie's place. Halo was the last one he drove home. She seemed to have sobered up a bit but said, "Not looking forward to the hangover tomorrow," before barely closing the passenger door and shuffling to her front entrance.

Silas eventually arrived at his own house and was about to get out of his truck when a buzzing sound emanated from the back seat. He searched and quickly spotted the glowing screen of a forgotten smartphone.

"Hello?" he said, answering the call.

"Dammit," Raven's voice said on the other line. "I left my phone in your car, didn't I?"

"Yeah, looks like it."

There was a big sigh before she said, "All right, I'll pick it up tomorrow."

"It's okay. I can drop it off now. I'll be there soon."

Chapter Seventeen

WHEN RAVEN REALIZED she didn't have her phone, she assumed she'd left it at the concert venue—it wouldn't have been the first time. But the reality was more inconvenient, Silas had it, and he was coming over to return it.

"Coming over" was a little dramatic because it would only be a quick transfer. Hell, she could probably get away with sticking her hand out the door to retrieve it.

Raven stopped pacing the room to look at her reflection in the mirror beside the television console.

"Thank you," she said to herself, practicing for Silas's arrival. "Thanks! Appreciate it! Appreciate you!"

Jesus. This was embarrassing.

She took a seat in one of the chairs in the room, and not even a minute later, a loud knock sounded at her door. She looked through the peephole and saw Silas's face in fisheye distortion before opening the door wider than she'd promised herself she would.

The breeze behind Silas pushed the scent of the subtle woodsy cologne he wore toward her. It beckoned her closer.

"Here you go," he said, holding out her phone.

"Thank you. I appreciate you coming back all this way."

"No problem. Have a good night," he said, turning to leave, and she thought she'd just survived the moment, but then Silas stopped and returned to the spot in front of her. "Actually, I want to talk to you about something."

It was one in the morning, and whatever he had to say could probably wait, but with a suddenly dry throat Raven said, "What's up?"

"We obviously have an attraction," he began. "There're conflicting priorities, though, so I think it's best if we keep things professional."

"I agree," Raven said, relieved. "I was planning to bring up that exact thing."

"Good, so we're on the same page," he said.

She nodded and opened her mouth to add something else but hesitated.

"What?" he asked.

"No, I was just thinking how it would be helpful if you stopped doing that eye thing you do."

"Eye thing?" he asked with a slight head shake.

"You get this smoldering intensity in your eyes every time we're about to kiss."

She'd essentially admitted that a mere look from him made her weak, but she wasn't centering her ego right now. All that mattered was they stopped making out.

"Okay, I'll try not to do that anymore," he said resolutely. "And since we're on the topic, you need to stop looking at my lips."

"I don't look at your lips," Raven said as heat warmed her cheeks.

He smiled slowly. "Yeah, you do. I might do that eye

thing, but you look at my lips every time we're about to kiss."

She'd opened this can of worms, but she was still embarrassed. "All right, I hear you," she said.

"Great," he replied, and she wished he'd immediately said good night and turned away instead of stand there for several beats because now that she'd agreed not to look at his lips, that's exactly want she wanted to do.

He did have beautiful lips that felt amazing wherever they landed.

"Raven," Silas said, his voice gruff.

She looked him in the eyes and found them hot like embers. And with the suddenness of a crack of lightning, they sprang to join their bodies for a passionate kiss. His tongue boldly stoked heat across her skin. He tasted good and smelled divine.

"We return to strictly professionals tomorrow," he said against her mouth.

"No weirdness or awkwardness," she replied, and their deal was sealed with another urgent kiss.

She pulled him deeper into her motel room, shutting the door with her foot. Shirts came off, hands found purchase in hair, and they stumbled through the space— bumping into furniture, leaving fallen items in their wake until Silas swept her into his arms and planted her on the edge of the table connected to the TV console.

With him standing between her open legs, her hands couldn't be stilled. They skimmed his strong arms, his sturdy chest, the raised scar that ran along his right shoulder, his soft belly. She liked that he wasn't ripped, that his strength didn't require sculpted muscles.

His lips traveled over her chin, cheeks, and down the length of her neck. He deftly removed her bra and sharply exhaled as he leaned back to study her. "Fuck, Raven."

The richness of his voice spurred her nipples before the soft strokes of his fingers over them sent a cascade of glittering pulses to her clit.

"This okay?" he asked as he gently tugged on her piercing, and her breath hitched as she nodded.

When he lowered his head to draw her pierced nipple in his mouth, she gasped, taking hold of the coils on his head. He worked his tongue around and around her nipples, and Raven caressed his hardening dick where it pressed against the front of his pants.

Her fondling eventually drove Silas to straighten and recapture her lips in a kiss. She unbuttoned his jeans, and he shoved them down along with his boxer briefs. Sparks scattered to the sensitive points of her body as she took him in.

"I want to suck you off," she said, nudging him backward. She hopped off the table and pushed him until he was seated on the edge of her bed.

"Fuck," he whispered as she dropped to her knees in front of him.

She took his dick in her hand, and a breathless excitement engulfed her as she explored its weight and girth.

"You good?" Silas asked with a half smile, but the moment her mouth touched his thick tip, his expression went slack.

She licked and teased him, mimicking the lazy kisses he'd given her across her face and breasts.

"You look incredible," he whispered, brushing his thumb over her top lip that was stretched around his head. It was just the encouragement she needed to fill her mouth with more of him.

The contours of his hardened length pressed against her tongue, crowded her cheeks. Rough moans rolled out of him, and his hand found a place on the back of her head.

"That's it, get it nice and hard for me," he said, gently guiding her.

Her eyes flickered upward, and she found him looking at her. A flutter crossed her chest. But to avoid analyzing the feeling, she planted her hands on Silas's thighs and quickened her movements.

His moans grew desperate and stirred her lust. She slipped her hand down the front of her underwear to give her needy clit a few taps and strokes.

"Sucking my dick turns you on, huh? Show me how wet you are," he whispered, and Raven ran her fingers down her slit before drawing them out for him to see how they glistened.

A harsh breath escaped him as he pulled his dick from her mouth and said, " I need to bury my face in your pussy. Back on the table."

She quickly followed the command, and he rewarded her by pushing her tight skirt over her hips to expose her thighs and the front of her damp underwear.

"This all you're wearing under there?" he asked her, his voice strained.

"A thong? Yes."

"It barely covers you," he said, dragging his knuckles over her pussy.

"That's the point," she said, amused. "You must've seen a thong before."

He smiled at her. The sort of playful smile that comes when you've fucked someone a few times and you know their body.

When he dropped to his knees, he pushed her legs wide. From her place above, she watched him shove the material of her underwear to expose her pussy to the air, his breath, his gaze. A moan from the back of his throat tumbled out as he studied her. She didn't want to breathe or blink, lest she miss something.

He parted her folds with his fingers. "Fuck, you've got such a pretty clit."

The kiss he planted on her sensitive bud unleashed the most glorious feeling in her body. He introduced his tongue, and she slipped into the sweet embrace of pleasure.

"Silas, please," she whimpered. Her request was undefined, nebulous, but somehow he knew what she needed. He eased two fingers inside of her, pitching her into a different gear of arousal. With each move he made, her focus narrowed.

She grabbed his hair in a fist. "God, right there."

His warm tongue, his wide lips, the slightly abrasive beard, and the fingers he drove in and out of her were pushing her closer and closer to her end. She braced herself against the furniture as if her soul might launch from her chest.

"I'm gonna come all over your beard," she said, to which he responded by holding her fast against his face. She bucked and cried out incoherent words. There was nowhere to go but up, so she yielded to the ascent until she saw the constellations rearrange before her eyes.

———

Raven lounged on the bed with her head propped up in a hand, watching Silas put on a condom. The only condom he had in his wallet.

He stroked himself to dull the edge that was building within. She looked at him with such awe; the corner of her bottom lip caught between her teeth. He wanted to bask in it. Lean back and allow her her fill.

If this wasn't just a one-time thing, he would have wanted to watch her masturbate, see her fingers slide across her clit, tease herself into a cresting orgasm.

"Silas," she said, her voice husky.

"Growing impatient?" he asked as he walked to the bed, flipping her onto her back and dragging her by the hips to the edge of the mattress.

She looked stunning lying there. Her dark skin contrasted against the white sheets and made her look like she was floating on clouds.

Her legs had fallen open, revealing her folds slick from his work with his tongue and her desire.

Everything in him wanted to surge into her and release them both from this aching suspension. But he also wanted them to savor this moment. He wanted to fuck her so good that they were both satisfied and didn't need to do this again.

He placed himself before her, moving one of her shapely legs so that it lay straight against his chest. While kissing the smooth skin of her calf, he dragged his dick along her pussy.

"How much dick do you want?" he asked as he guided just the tip inside of her. "This good?"

"More," she whispered.

He eased himself farther inside, watching her plump folds part for him. "This enough?"

She shook her head, her eyes half-mast.

"Now?" he rasped after giving her a little more of him.

"Silas, please just fuck me," she said desperately, clutching his forearms.

And his paper-thin restraint finally broke.

He pulled his dick from her before driving back in to

the hilt. The responding gasp and the way her breasts and soft belly shook had his balls tightening.

Her mouth fell open as he withdrew and returned with a harder stroke, and he wished he could escape the image of her right now. That he could wake up without it chiseled into the walls of his skull, but he knew it would be. Just like he knew the sound she'd make on his next thrust into her pussy.

"You feel so good," she said to him in a honeyed voice, her hands climbing above her head, as if in a stretch. Her braids spilling around her arms.

So fucking pretty. So fucking sexy.

He began a pace that would have her shaking, him sweating, and their bodies slapping to an unrelenting rhythm.

"You're a screamer, huh?" he asked as her moans became louder and more unbridled with each stroke.

"Can't. Be. Too. Loud," she said.

"Scared the neighbors gonna hear you getting absolutely fucked?"

She nodded, her face tense in concentration.

No, he needed her to feel and express everything, uninhibited by the sensibilities of whoever was on the other side of the wall.

He removed his dick from her gripping heat, cutting short her build. She wailed in protest. It felt like dropping out of heaven, but he'd get them back there.

"Get on your hands and knees for me," he said, and she scrambled to the setup. He drew in a breath at the swell of hips, gliding beautifully to her narrower waist. She looked at him with a dreamy smile over her shoulder, and something in his chest ballooned.

Terms of endearment wanted to spring out of his

mouth, but that felt too intimate—a violation of their casual night together.

With his hands gripping her ample hips, Silas entered her slowly and began working her up and down his length.

"Oh, God," she shouted into the pillow as her ass lewdly slapped against his pelvis over and over again.

He splayed his arm across the front of her body, hauling her up to his chest. Her head fell back on his shoulder, and he kissed the side of her heated cheek and temple.

"You're taking my dick so well," he said against her ear as he continued thrusting.

"I want to come," she whispered, so he spat on his fingers and found her clit. He chased bliss, stroking Raven past the point where her mouth dropped open and her eyes rolled back.

When she finally came, it was with her sweet pussy gripping him and a sound that resonated through the room. He found his glorious end on a wave of her moans.

Chapter Eighteen

RAVEN WOKE up to a deliciously sated body. She stretched her achy limbs, smiling as she recalled how the evening had unfolded. Turning, she looked to the other side of the bed but found it empty, only realizing she'd hoped for a different reality when her stomach did a somersault.

"Stop it," she told herself.

And she hopped out of bed, picking up her clothes on her way to the bathroom. A bathroom that was warm and filled with condensation, meaning Silas had left within the last half an hour.

He'd spent the entire night with her.

God, she wished she'd slept a little less soundly so she could remember the cuddling.

As she stepped into the shower, she thought about how her night with Silas hadn't felt like the other hookups she'd had in the past. He'd paid attention to her in a way that had been a little unnerving. She was used to hot and lustful. But she wasn't used to tender.

It had been difficult not to extrapolate in those

moments. To picture a reality where she could revel in those feelings again and again.

Once out of the shower, Raven was moisturizing when she froze suddenly, registering the TV playing in the next room. She'd not turned it on. She quickly threw on her robe and picked up her blow dryer, cursing herself for not bringing her phone to the bathroom.

"Hello?" she called out before she rounded the corner, ready to bonk a head if needed.

"Hey, morning!"

Silas.

Raven immediately relaxed hearing his voice and placed her weapon down before fully entering the room. He was dressed in yesterday's clothes but nevertheless looked refreshed.

"I was getting us some breakfast at the Yodeling Loon," he said, turning to look at her. "Didn't want to wake you."

His eyes traveled the length of her body, and the delicate parts he'd explored responded as if he'd touched her. But she ignored the call to jump all over him and instead approached the table he'd set up with food.

"This is really nice, thank you," she said, taking in the pancakes, bacon, fruit medley, and coffee.

As they took their seats, Raven felt nervous about sharing a meal with him. They did it every day, sure, but not after sex.

"What are you thinking about?" he asked as he passed her utensils.

"Just how it's kinda wild that you had your face between my thighs hours ago, but now I don't know if putting my legs in your lap would be too much."

She added a laugh at the end to soften her words and hopefully lessen the possibility of them coming off as a serious request. But Silas studied her, then bent over and lifted her feet into his lap without another word.

Her cheeks warmed, and it took a beat to fully relax and dig into her breakfast like he was doing. They ate in comfortable silence, and Raven watched Silas stretch his right arm, rotating and massaging the shoulder.

"I hope I didn't hurt you," she said.

"How would you have hurt me?"

"Well, you did toss me around a lot, and I wasn't very gentle."

He smiled shamelessly, and she was grateful to be seated because her knees would have certainly buckled.

"I'm made of stronger stuff," he said. "But my shoulder is always tight in the morning. I do stretches to keep it nimble."

"From the accident?" she asked.

"Yeah, that definitely made it worse. But generally, archers have to stay on top of our shoulder and back health."

"How long did it take for you to recover?" she asked.

"Nine weeks before I could start training again," he said, his eyes dimming.

"Sorry, I didn't mean to bring up a painful memory," she said.

"Nah, you good," he said, his hand mindlessly rubbing her calf. "It should've been more like six weeks, but I'd lost a respectable endorsement deal and my manager had dropped me. I was in a bad place."

"Understandable," she replied softly. "I'm happy you got through it eventually."

"It was actually Chuck who helped," Silas said, a sad smile appearing. "Everyone's pity was so overwhelming. And just adding to my own self-pitying and anger. I'd worked at Mountaintop, running weekend classes over the years, so Chuck had come to visit me at my place."

Silas laughed then, actually seeming happy.

"Everyone would enter my house all scared and shit, ask me how I was, then tell me I looked good—I didn't. But Chuck came in and saw me on the couch, watching TV, and said, 'Oh.'"

"That's it?" Raven asked.

"Yup. No sympathetic pats on the back, no gentle encouragement, no tough love. It was just the weight of that 'oh'—it felt like he was asking me, 'So this is it for you, huh?' It felt like something other than resentment to latch on to. It made therapy and physio not feel like a waste of time. It basically made recovery easier."

Her understanding of the part Mountaintop played in his life deepened.

"Chuck seemed like a great man," Raven said, swallowing hard. "And I'm sorry for your loss. I don't think I've said that before."

He responded with a gentle squeeze to her ankle, and they finished their breakfasts with lighter conversation. To Raven, the end of the meal felt like the start of a slow morning where a visit to the farmers' market would follow, then a leisurely lunch they'd prepare together. But that was a fantasy in her head, so she got up and started clearing the table.

Silas straightened up the general room, repositioning furniture they'd shifted last night.

"Oh, you can just put that on the nightstand," she told him when he held up some of her crystals that had fallen on the floor.

"It's amethyst, right?" he said, raising it to the light to study it further. "For calm, peace. And restful sleep."

"Wait, I didn't know you were into crystals," she said,

smiling when he started rubbing the stone between his hands.

"I'm not, but I was a little curious after we pulled off that heist at the Crawleys, so I looked into them," he said with a shrug.

It wasn't a big deal. Or it shouldn't have been, but Raven was strangely delighted. She'd had boyfriends who'd never even cared to ask her about her spiritual rituals or interests, let alone research it on their own time. And though intellectually she knew Silas hadn't looked up crystals specifically for her, she was charmed.

"Okay, I'll let you get on with your day," he said once all was cleared.

"Thanks for breakfast," she said, walking him to the door.

"No problem," he replied before catching her off guard by giving her the gentlest kiss.

It left her breathless, and she stared after him as he exited.

———

"You look rough," Silas said when Halo opened her front door with one eye closed and hair in disarray. "I got you some breakfast, though."

"Bless you," she said, taking the bag he held and waving him inside.

"Can't stay long, just wanted to drop this off," he said, following her into the kitchen, where she arranged herself at the breakfast nook amidst a stack of dusty cookbooks and a dried-up bouquet.

"Today's worth living," she said when she opened the box holding the cinnamon bun. She then gave him another look from his place against the counter. "You're wearing the same thing from last night."

"No, I'm not," he said quickly.

"Yeah, you are because I remember being bothered by that crease in your T-shirt half the night."

He shrugged, not caring to explain himself, but Halo continued to study him. "You were with Raven."

This sent his head snapping backward. "What?"

"I might look rough, but you look like you didn't spend the night sleeping."

"Wow, okay," Silas said, rubbing his neck.

"What does that mean? You guys an item?" Halo asked as she forked a big piece of cinnamon bun into her mouth.

"No!"

She raised her hands. "Just a question. We all can see something is going on between you two."

"What? Who is we?"

"Me, Doc, and Bodie. Hell, even my daughter. We see the flirting. The way she looks at you. How nervous you get when she enters a room. It's like watching an old computer reboot." The older woman launched into a series of staccato body movements to underscore her point and, in the process, left Silas feeling embarrassed that the feelings he'd thought he had expertly concealed had been so obvious.

"Regardless of how it may seem, I can promise you it's nothing serious," he told Halo. "It's only attraction."

He could admit, however, that eating breakfast with Raven had felt comfortable, as evidenced by the story he'd told her about Chuck's role in his surgery recovery. She was only the second person he'd ever shared that with. Her warm nature made it easy to share things with her.

"I like her for what it's worth," Halo said around the food she chewed.

"That's a one-eighty for you," Silas said.

"I'm a judgmental woman—some might call me a bitch—but I can admit when I'm wrong. And Raven—I don't know how to describe it, but she does everything with an intensity I appreciate."

Silas nodded, knowing exactly what she meant.

"Don't worry, though," Halo swiftly added. "I might've warmed up to her, but I'll always want you heading Mountaintop. I still think she'll get bored of this place."

It was true. Raven had her arms wide open to embrace life and experiences, and Cedar was too easily grasped.

"Do you ever get tired of Cedar?" Silas asked Halo, surprising himself with the question.

"No, never. It's a slow life I crave."

It was a sentiment shared by many townspeople.

"And you?" Halo asked. "You like living in Cedar?"

"Yeah, it's home," he said easily enough.

He could see himself living in all sorts of places, and sometimes he thought about how coaching competitive archers destined for podiums would afford him that opportunity. But it didn't seem like a desperate enough calling to abandon what he had going on in Cedar.

In Cedar, he was close to his family, had a beautiful home, and was around people he enjoyed working with. He was content.

Chapter Nineteen

THE TIME HAD COME. Chestnut the squirrel had completely healed. It was safe for him to return home now that the splint was gone. Bodie had insisted they needed a ceremony to send the animal off, so the entire Mountaintop team stood in front of the cabin early in the morning on a workday to say farewell.

"This will be goodbye, my friend," Bodie said to Chestnut, who'd been placed before them for the direct address. "Hopefully not forever. You can visit whenever."

The buff man bowed his head and asked, "Anyone want to say a few words? Silas?"

Raven peeked over at Silas, who seemed to have gotten no heads-up about the speech he was supposed to deliver. He looked so handsome even when floundering.

"Whenever you're ready, Silas," Doc said with a playful nudge to Silas's side, and Raven had to turn her head before she burst out laughing.

Silas eventually cleared his throat and said, "Chestnut, you are incredibly agile. In fact, it's the reason you broke your leg. Falling out of a tree. That was sad, but now you're better and get to leave... Congrats."

"Anyone else?" Bodie asked, his head still bent as if in prayer.

Doc stepped forward and said, "It was fun having you around, bud."

"Best of luck," Halo offered afterward with a salute.

Since everyone had given a word, Raven felt compelled to as well. "You made my arrival in Cedar Lake memorable, and I thank you for that."

Bodie removed Chestnut from his crate and placed him on the ground. The rodent took a tentative step forward, testing the limits of his freedom, before wasting no time and scurrying away.

"There he goes," Bodie said.

An unexpected melancholy swelled within Raven as she watched the squirrel pause at the edge of the forest and turn back to look at them before disappearing into the woods.

"Okay, time to get on with the day, folks," Silas said with a clap.

As the group headed back to the cabin, laughing and talking about the day ahead, Raven couldn't shake off the sadness. That silly but adorable moment had made her feel more like a part of Mountaintop Adventures than anything previously, and something in her knew she'd never be able to recapture it.

They still viewed Silas as their leader-in-waiting. It was apparent in how they had just deferred to him to kick off the speeches and how they still needed him to cosign minor policies she implemented.

If she decided to stay, they'd grow to resent her. The friendliness that had been cultivated between her and Silas would also crumble.

The last reality made her chest grow tight.

"You good?" Silas asked her when they got inside. "Not too torn up about Chestnut, I hope."

Could he read her face? Raven managed a light laugh despite her tongue feeling thick and her throat dry.

She quickly retreated to her place behind the reception desk where Libby was already parked nearby with her summer schoolwork.

For the next hour, Raven greeted clients who came in and attempted to do some administrative tasks, but she grew too distracted to be any sort of productive. Raven left her post for the restroom, pulling out her phone when she was locked inside.

The moment her best friend picked up, Raven blurted, "I'm falling for Silas."

"Oh, okay," Gwen said, chuckling. "I'm not going to say it's a total surprise the way you've—"

"Also, I'm leaving," Raven said.

"Wait, what?"

"I'm going to sell the business to Silas, then come home."

"I literally thought you were about to tell me you'd decided to stay and move in with him or something," her friend said, and it was a reasonable assumption since Raven had done it before to heartbreaking effect.

"I'm finally applying the accumulated lessons," Raven responded.

"Isn't this a little drastic, though? You were excited about the possibilities of Mountaintop."

Her heart was involved now. It would spoil things. She'd known sleeping with Silas was a bad idea, that it would deepen her feelings, but she'd done it anyway.

"My mom once said that when I get really into someone, it's like those eighties commercials that show the difference between a brain on and off drugs."

"Okay, I'm not following," Gwen said.

"What I'm saying is that I've ignored my intuition and overstayed in Cedar because of him. First to spite him, then because I liked him." She was never supposed to be some queenpin of an outdoorsy tourism company.

"So you're listening to your gut by leaving?" her friend asked.

"Yes," Raven said, but she wasn't entirely sure that was the truth. She'd always described her intuition as a nudge —a suggestion as intrusive as a breeze. The feelings rolling inside her were more pressing, a siren urging her to run.

"At least you'll get the money," Gwen said.

"Exactly, nothing lost," Raven said with a confidence that should've been more robust considering the momentous decision she'd just made.

———

Silas studied one green paint swatch before looking at another that was almost identical in color. He kept changing his mind from one second to the next which he preferred.

"It's a tough choice," Walt, the shop owner, said from his position next to Silas.

"I feel like I'm going to end up painting the wall white at this rate," Silas said.

"The nice thing about paint is you can change it if you don't like it."

It was such a good reminder that it jolted Silas out of his indecision. "Okay, I'm going with this one," Silas said, presenting the old man with the swatch with a slightly more yellow tinge.

"Great choice, son," Walt said before marching to the back to mix the paint.

Meanwhile, Silas picked up a few other items, including a new three-inch flat paint brush with a handle that matched the pink polish Raven had been wearing on her nails this week. He shook his head as if it might physically dislodge the errant thought.

As Walt rang up Silas's items at the register, the man leaned close and said, "I heard about Mountaintop. The new owner. I'm sorry."

"Things are still up in the air. It's not a for sure thing," Silas said halfheartedly. It had become a well-used phrase over the past month.

The old man looked surprised by Silas's correction. "Is that so? I heard she's been looking at homes around town."

"Where did you hear that from?"

It was probably conjecture. Cedar gossip was stoked by people trying to have the biggest news to reveal, which naturally encouraged hyperbole. Not to mention the game of telephone that happened that resulted in some weird stories.

"Yeah, it's true." Walt nodded eagerly before shouting, "Caroline!"

His wife, a plump woman of fifty, walked out from the backroom.

"What I tell you about yelling for me like that? I'm not a dog," Caroline said.

"Sorry, honey, but Silas here's asking where you heard about the new girl looking for a home."

The woman's eyes lit up as she turned to him. "Mrs. Zimmer told me that Raven was seen leaving a house viewing last weekend."

"She saw this firsthand?" Silas asked.

"Well, no. Her son is dating Ashley Pham, who's

friends with Beth Chamberlin, who's looking for a new home now that she and Gavin have that second baby on the way. They saw Raven at the house viewing."

In his mind's eye, Silas always tried to see the entire situation working out in his favor. But if Raven was looking for homes, it meant she was leaning toward staying.

"Thanks for letting me know," Silas said before leaving the store. When he got into his truck, he placed the keys in the ignition but didn't go anywhere. He stared, unseeing, at the cars rolling along Main Street, his brain fixated on one question: What if Raven stayed?

The thought previously would've spurred a spike of anxiety and some fretting. He'd told his brother weeks ago that he wasn't going to even think about it yet, but today it was a question that he wanted to investigate.

If Raven stayed, she'd most likely remain the boss and continue to be great at it. Despite the disruption her presence had initially caused, there was no denying she was an asset to Mountaintop.

Also, Silas had grown accustomed to her; he liked seeing her around the cabin handling one project or another. That said, they would have to refrain from exploring their attraction further for professionalism's sake.

But if Raven stayed, what would he do?

The answer presumably was continue teaching introductory archery classes to tourists and a few locals. That filled him with dread.

Owning Mountaintop was supposed to bring him a new level of satisfaction. It was the accomplishment meant to appease his ambition and soothe any lingering disappointment in the direction of his life post-injury.

If Raven stayed, Silas didn't know if there was a space for him here. And if that were true, where the hell would he go?

Chapter Twenty

RAVEN HAD SPENT her weekend holed up in her motel room trying to figure out how to break the news that she was leaving Cedar Lake. It was days after she'd made the decision, but she'd yet to inform Silas and the rest of the Mountaintop team.

She was self-aware enough to know she was stalling to avoid the moment when she would witness Silas's face light up at the thought of her departure.

To combat complacency and force herself to finally reveal the news, Raven had approached Silas that morning and told him she needed to speak with him at the end of the day.

Now she was accountable. There was no way to back out of it. Unless she died. Which was a possibility since soon she'd be rappelling down a twenty-foot cliff along with eight other newbies in Halo's Rappelling 101 class.

"You will be defying gravity today," Halo said to the group, pacing as if she were a sergeant. "The rope that will help you achieve this can hold up to three thousand pounds. Trust in it."

There was a swirl of excitement and nerves among participants as Halo's daughter, who'd been put in charge of carrying the first aid kit and helping her mom facilitate the lesson, handed out the gear.

"Do we really need to wear helmets?" someone asked.

"No," Halo said bluntly. "As long as you're okay with cracking your skull against the rock formation."

And that was enough for the tourist to plop the protective headwear on her head and fasten it tightly.

Throughout Halo's introduction and lesson, Raven went back and forth on whether to participate or sit out. She made her final decision after watching Libby, only fifteen, and a man in his sixties descend the steep slope. How could she not at least attempt it?

When Halo approached Raven to check the placement of her harness and carabiners, the older woman must've seen Raven eyeing the trees the rope was being anchored to and said, "They're healthy. Green leaves, deep roots, strong bark. You're safe."

She sounded so assured that it worked to allay Raven's nerves. That didn't mean when it was her turn, she didn't shake while standing backward at the cliff's edge.

"Lean back," Halo said.

Fighting against all human instinct, Raven, while holding her breath, took a step. Her hold around the rope tightened as she felt herself drop. Her back now faced the forest ground below.

However, she was still in suspension, so she started moving her feet over the perpendicular surface, not allowing her mind to ruminate too long on the activity she was participating in. The harness cut into her body, but she appreciated the discomfort because it let her know she was being supported.

"That's it. Go as slow as you need to," Halo said from

above. Her voice had grown more distant, giving Raven another indication that she was moving and not floating in place.

Halfway, she started to embrace the feeling of being above the earth. She still didn't look down or loosen her grip, but she decided to take stock of the moment.

Amongst the clouds and the treetops, Raven felt sort of free, and for the remainder of her journey to solid ground, all her worries momentarily fell away.

"You did it!" a woman said at the bottom, and Raven hugged the woman whose name she didn't know.

She rappelled two more times with increasing confidence every turn. It left her invigorated, and at the end of class, the daunting parts of her life, namely the conversation she was about to have with Silas, didn't seem so bad.

She took the back of the group on the walk to the cabin, in step with Libby who'd returned to her phone.

"Crap," the teen said, stopping in her tracks. "I forgot the first aid kit at the site."

"Keep going. I'll go grab it," Raven said, turning back to speed-walk the few minutes to the cliff. She spotted the bright red kit leaning against a tree long before she'd reached it.

Once she'd slung the bag across her shoulder, Raven set on the straightforward path out of the woods. But when, out of habit, she reached for her citrine pendant and didn't find it around her neck, she stopped.

Raven palmed her collarbone, neck, and chest, then looked down at her clothes, hoping to find the necklace caught on her jeans or the pocket of her lightweight jacket. She searched the ground around her for the amber stone, shoving aside the dirt and leaves with the toe of her boot.

She'd definitely put it on that morning. Or had she? She'd been a bit distracted the last few days. Maybe she was misremembering one of the other times she'd worn it. No, she'd been playing with it that morning while on hold with the electrical company.

But there was no way, if she did lose her necklace out here, that she'd spot it amidst similarly colored foliage. It wasn't an heirloom, at least. She'd bought the necklace in a store in New Orleans years ago; she'd get another.

With that unideal conclusion, Raven abandoned her search to resume her trek to the cabin. She retraced her steps toward the trail she'd departed from but soon paused.

"Wait..." she said out loud, looking to her left and right. When she didn't immediately know which direction to go, a sliver of panic pricked the base of her spine.

"Focus, Raven. It was a straight line."

She scanned the trees, looking for trail signs but found them bare.

"Fuck me," she mumbled. She couldn't have gone that off course.

She walked between the trees and over shrubbery in one direction, hoping to stumble across a cleared path. But everything looked like everything else, and she failed to orient herself.

"Shit. Shit. Shit," Raven said, dread pushing her to move quickly between the trees as if speed alone was preventing her from finding her way. Adrenaline was sharpening the sounds around her to the pitch of an off-tune orchestra.

No, this couldn't be happening. There was no way.

She stopped her frantic bumbling and pressed her back against a tree, taking strategic inhales and exhales from her nose until the fear receded to a manageable level.

Raven took a fresh look at the labyrinthine forest around her and concluded, "Okay. All right. I'm lost."

Her thoughts were reaching for her next move, but panic was battling for dominance.

"Think, Raven. Think."

She'd gotten lost tons of times. But those moments had been in big cities where she could dip into a small store and ask for directions or use her phone.

Phone.

She pulled out her cell. There was no service, but the time let her know she'd been lost for less than ten minutes. Not that bad, right? She couldn't have walked too far.

Weeks ago, Doc had mentioned what to do in this type of situation. Find a river—no, she had to stay put. Yes, someone from Mountaintop would notice she was missing.

Raven took a step backward to scope out the best possible spot to sit and wait, but her feet slipped from under her. She landed hard on the ground, and before she could attempt to sit up, she began to roll down a hill.

Raven grabbed at the leaves and the roots as she tumbled, trying to stop her trajectory. However, it was futile as she continued gaining speed. All she could do was cover her head and wait for what would meet her at the bottom.

————

Silas had just locked the door to the cabin behind the last customer of the day when he turned to look at the empty reception desk. His scheduled talk with Raven had been simmering in his head all day, and he wanted to get it over with.

He had no idea what she wanted to discuss, but something told him it wouldn't be a casual conversation. Ever since he found out Raven had been looking at homes, he'd been waiting for the other shoe to drop.

He straightened the chairs in the waiting area and double-checked the bathroom for straggling customers before heading to the break room. Upon entering, Silas scanned the room for Raven, but she wasn't there. She'd arrive any moment, he reasoned.

"Whoever is responsible for that nasty yogurt growing a colony in the fridge, do something about it," Halo said to the room.

"That's Bodie's," Doc said.

"No, it's not," Bodie replied before the two men commenced a breakdown of who ate what flavor of yogurt.

As Silas packed up his belongings, he kept looking up, expecting to see Raven. While refilling his water bottle, he peeked out of the door to see if he could spot her in the main area of the cabin. No luck.

The debate of whose yogurt was stinking up the fridge continued as Silas dipped out of the kitchen to check the storage closet. He found it dark and empty. And because he was nearby, he also rechecked the restroom to dismal results.

"Anyone seen Raven?" Silas asked when he returned to the break room.

Halo looked around the kitchen as if she hadn't noticed she was missing. "Probably in the washroom."

"No, I was just there," Silas said.

"Maybe she left already," Bodie offered.

Silas nodded to Raven's stuff on the counter. "Her purse is still here."

Also, the team usually congregated outside before leaving in succession.

"She was in my last rappelling class of the day. I definitely saw her while we were walking back from the site," Halo said before tapping her daughter's shoulder.

"What?" the teen asked, peeling her headphone from an ear.

"You walked in with Raven after my class, right?"

"No," Libby said, straightening in her seat. "I forgot the first aid kit, and she went back to the cliff to get it."

"Did you see her come back?" Silas asked as something slow but persistent began to press at his chest.

"I thought she did," the teen said, pointing to a first aid kit sitting on the counter.

"That one's mine," Doc said, and the atmosphere shifted with those words.

Something was wrong.

"I'll check the shed," Bodie said, leaving the room.

Silas pulled out his phone and called Raven's number while he retrieved the search-and-rescue packs from a low cupboard. Meanwhile, Doc and Halo opened a map on the table.

"What site did you rappel at today?" Doc asked.

"Site A," Halo replied, running her hands through her short hair.

Bodie returned from searching the shed and simply shook his head. Panic wanted to tear through the surface of Silas's skin, but he slammed it down, not letting himself think further than the next steps.

"All right," Silas said to the team. "Her phone is going straight to voicemail. She's probably still out there with no service." He swallowed hard before continuing. "Doc and I will go search the site. If she returns, radio us. And if we're still gone when the sun sets, call the constable."

With everyone briefed on their roles, Silas left the cabin with Doc for Site A.

Most people got lost at the beginning or at the end of a trail, so Silas had to force himself to slow down, look, and listen. There was no wisdom in racing; he'd risk missing her. Every few minutes, he'd called out her name.

When the men arrived at the site, they didn't see a first aid kit.

"We know she got the kit, so she must've gotten lost on the way back," Doc said.

It was helpful, but it didn't ease his heart palpitations.

"Raven!" Silas called out once and stilled to listen for a response that did not come.

And when Doc walked to the edge of the cliff and looked over, Silas stopped breathing until Doc turned around and shook his head. A dizzying relief flooded him, but shit wasn't over.

"Okay, we take a four-quadrant approach and meet back here," Silas said before they split up to execute the search strategy. He looked for classic signs of disruption. Broken branches, trampled foliage. Anything that could indicate where Raven had trodden.

But his search yielded nothing, and time passed quicker than he could make ground. The sun was dipping, and the forest was getting darker.

"Where are you, Raven?" he whispered anxiously, struggling with the fear stabbing him. But then, from deep in the woods, Doc shouted, "I found something!"

———

"I am grateful for the sun. And I'm grateful for the Double Stuf Oreos in my motel room that I'll eat when I definitely get out of here alive. I have flint, so I can make fire if I need to," Raven said aloud.

She was sitting up against a boulder and doing her best to keep her mind occupied so it wouldn't roam to the bleakest of places.

After she'd landed at the bottom of the hill, Raven had lain on the forest floor, staring at the tops of the pine trees and the blue that peeked through, trying to gauge how fucked she was. Adrenaline had still been coursing through her, making it difficult to discern anything past her own breathing and the relentless pound of her heart.

But when she'd settled, she noted there was no pain and she couldn't smell the metallic bite of blood. The pain, however, roared when she'd tried to stand. Her left ankle couldn't handle any weight; climbing the hill she'd fallen down was out of the question. So she'd crawled to the boulder she sat against now—dragging her injured limb behind her and forgiving the dirt for settling painfully underneath her nails.

A few times along the way, she collapsed to the ground to catch her breath and wipe the sweat stinging her eyes. But she'd finally got there. And now she had some security. Something to cower behind if a wild animal—

"I am grateful that I didn't smash my head on the way down. I'm grateful for *Love Island*. And I'm grateful that I have this first aid kit," she said before swallowing hard to relieve her dry mouth without touching her waning water supply.

As much as she was trying to remain positive, Raven was also trying to prepare for a scenario that would see her spending the night in the woods. She doubted she could fall asleep; her ears were too concerned with the noises emanating from the forest to really relax.

She skimmed her hands over the supplies she'd neatly displayed next to her. Taking inventory was soothing. Twelve ounces of water, flint, a smartphone with 30 percent battery life, and a first aid kit with immediately relevant items like a space blanket and a pocketknife.

The Mountaintop staff had to have noticed she was

missing by now. It was close to an hour since she gotten lost. They'd have gathered outside in the parking area to bid each other a good evening before leaving, and Silas would have noticed her absence. He was observant. And they'd planned to talk after work today.

He was most likely already out here. She could picture his furrowed brow and resolute lip as he whacked the bushes in search of her. Her heart danced at the idea. How foolish to conjure a fairy tale at a time like this, she thought.

An hour and a half into being lost, Raven caught an odd sound off in the distance and froze. A voice or a tree creaking? She closed her eyes and held her breath to focus.

Nothing.

Oh, she was losing it, and the sun hadn't even set.

Two hours in, she decided it wouldn't hurt to periodically call out into the thicket, "Help!" The response each time was the hum of nature.

Exhaustion soon started pressing her body.

"Don't fall asleep," she said to herself as her eyelids grew heavy, but she found herself, some time later, jerking awake. "Fuck."

The sun was dipping low, casting creeping shadows on the ground.

She could not doze off and risk missing help passing by. But her placement made it easy to fall asleep, so Raven gathered all the strength she could muster, and with the aid of the giant rock at her back, she hoisted herself to stand.

Her injured ankle throbbed like a second heartbeat to the point where only a few minutes later she regretted making the move.

"To sit or not to sit, that is the question," she said, immediately laughing at her unfunny joke. But she cut herself short when a sudden sound reached her ears.

It was different from everything she'd been hearing. It was human.

"Help!" she screamed. "Over here, I'm over here!"

Her scratchy throat cracked on the words, which wouldn't carry past the wall of trees in front of her. Raven dropped to the ground, ignoring the pain shooting up her leg, and rummaged through the first aid kit for the whistle she'd seen. With shaky hands, she pressed the whistle to her lips and blew like nothing else in the world mattered.

She blew even when her head started pounding and even when she began feeling woozy. She blew until she saw Silas, determined and strong, appear over the embankment she'd rolled down.

Chapter Twenty-One

THE FIRST TIME Silas ever felt real fear was the day he lost control of his ATV and went careening forward. The air had been knocked out of him, and a searing pain in his shoulder almost made him pass out.

The second time Silas felt real fear was when he saw Raven at the bottom of the hill, collapsing to the ground along with her whistle.

They should've found her sooner.

He bounded down the hill, Doc right behind him. When Silas reached her and found her eyes wet and chin trembling, he felt like he'd been split open. He tried to wipe her tears with the pads of his fingers, but they were too shaky to be effective.

"I'm so happy to see you guys. I wasn't ready to become a Tarzan rip-off," she said, laughing.

Her voice was hoarse, but hearing her laugh smoothed out the fear enough to where he could ask, "You okay? You in pain? Where does it hurt?"

"My ankle," she said. "I think I broke or sprained it while falling down that hill."

Again, she laughed, but Silas quite literally wanted to throw up.

"We'll head to the clinic," he told her as he removed twigs and leaves caught in her hair.

"It's a two-mile walk to the cabin from here," Doc said while gathering the items Raven had strewn on the ground.

"I'll carry you," Silas said, unconcerned that his bad shoulder was fatigued from a long day.

"Oh, no, please. I can walk. I'll just need your help," she said.

And though he wanted to insist, he let it go because the most important thing was getting her to the clinic.

He helped her stand and drape her arm across his shoulder. "Lean on me as much as you want," he told her as they began the tedious journey up the hill. Every wince from her prompted Silas to pull her in tighter against his body. By the time they reached the top, he was supporting most of her weight.

"Raven, let me just carry you on my back. I won't drop you," he said, and she must've really been tired and in pain because she didn't protest. He stooped low while she climbed on, and he held her firmly as he straightened, minding her injured foot.

With Raven's face nestled against his sweaty neck, her steady breathing kept him walking at a consistent pace, even when he grew tired and his shoulder began to throb.

When they finally emerged from the forest, the sun had mostly set, and only a dim orange glow could be seen on the horizon.

The Mountaintop team met them halfway in the field, their relief palpable. "I'm okay. Silas is taking me to the hospital," Raven assured Bodie before telling a guilt-ridden

Halo and her daughter, "It's not your fault! I'm the clumsy one."

All the while, Silas kept Raven on his back and didn't slow down until he'd reached his vehicle. He drove as carefully as he could, but every time he hit a bump in the road, he'd turn to look at her in the passenger seat.

"I'm good," she'd say, but it was a relief when they arrived at the small clinic.

Raven barely had to wait before she was ushered to the back for treatment. Silas, on the other hand, waited quite a while for her to return. In the interim, he paced the room, updated the team over text, stress-ate snacks from the vending machine, and tried not to replay the afternoon's events.

He was on his third bag of chips when Raven reappeared on crutches. Her left jean pant leg had been cut to capri length, and her foot was bandaged up.

"No head injury and it's just a sprain," she said, grinning. And once again, it was the simple fact that she was in good spirits that loosened the tightness in his lungs.

"I can't wait to take a shower. Eat something. Sleep," she said once they were back in his truck.

"What are you eating for dinner?" he asked as he pulled out of the parking lot.

"I have some Double Stuf Oreos that I'm pretty excited about," she said jokingly, but Silas cast her a look.

"I can make you some dinner," he said tentatively.

He thought she might reject his offer, but she said, "You know what? I'd love that."

And that's all he needed to change direction toward his own home.

———

"I always end up at your house in your clothes," Raven said, entering Silas's kitchen on her crutches and wearing his sweatshirt and pants. The last bits of stress he'd been harboring in his body melted away seeing the evidence of the day washed from her skin and hair.

Now that they were both showered, all that was left to do was eat.

"Food's almost done," he told her from his place in front of the stove. "You can take a seat while I finish up."

But she didn't listen and hobbled to stand beside him and peer into the pans. "It smells so good," she said.

"Carbonara," he told her.

When she didn't move to sit after that, he turned to look at her.

"Thanks for coming to find me," she said softly.

He swallowed. "I'm sorry you got lost."

"Not your fault," she said. "Got caught up looking for my necklace."

Silas had nearly forgotten.

"Hold on a second," he said as he quickly went over to his jacket and retrieved an item from the inside pocket before returning to Raven and presenting her with her citrine necklace. The clasp was broken, but overall it was still intact.

"How?" she asked, taking the jewelry carefully into her hands, amazement stark on her face.

"Doc found it tangled on a branch," he said. "It actually helped us find you by narrowing down the search area."

She shook her head, a smile lifting her lips. "Thank you," she said, and on the tail end of an exhale, she leaned in and kissed him. Silas wrapped his arms around her, feeling their heartbeats culminate in a thunderous roar between them.

"You should eat first," he said, trying to pull away, but she shook her head.

The pasta could wait.

Their warm tongues met on shortened breaths, and her hand across his heated skin felt like cool water lapping around him on a hot day. They walked to his bedroom, and once she was on the bed, she removed the sweatshirt she wore, exposing her naked body.

Breathtaking. A woman made to be lavished with adoration.

She grabbed him by his shoulders, dragging him on top of her. Keeping his weight off of her, Silas kissed her forehead, her eyelids, her nose, her lips before settling a few kisses on her neck. Her skin smelt of his shower gel and lotion, and for some reason, it turned him on.

His journey continued over her shoulders, across the swell of her breasts, her dark nipples. And when he reached her lower body, he slowly dragged his sweatpants off her.

He loved on her soft stomach, on the stretch marks he found on her hips and thighs. By the time he was on his knees between her spread legs, her breathing was coming out in shallow bursts.

He nuzzled the flesh of her thighs, relishing how the shower had warmed them up for him. As he progressed up her inner thigh, he could feel her inch closer to his face as if to hurry him along.

"Just relax, baby. I promise I'll make you feel good," he said, meeting her gaze.

"I know you will," she said breathlessly with a smile that made contact with his heart.

A light feeling accompanied him as he pressed a few kisses along her pussy. He wanted her to forget about all the bad parts of today.

When he parted her folds with his tongue, he quickly found her clit to gently suck and tease. Her moans filled the room, bouncing off the walls and encouraging his dick to harden against his pants.

"Oh, Silas," she whimpered as he eased two fingers inside her and began driving them in and out of her pussy.

She was so wet and eager, and after a time, he removed his fingers to simply hold her to his mouth and tongue-fuck her. He let Raven soak his chin, pull his hair, and chant his name.

And when she began thrashing against his face, he didn't relent until she was relaxed, sated.

———

He positioned them on their sides, pulling her back flush to his chest and enveloping her in his strong arms. He took care to mind her leg by draping it over his. His face was against her neck, nipping at her earlobe as he whispered how beautiful she was, how perfect her pussy was, how nice and slow he was about to fuck her.

By the time he got the condom on, she was aching for him. They moaned together as he entered her, filling her in a way that had her grabbing the sheets. He took his time sliding to the hilt.

The retreat of his dick was equally, deliciously slow, and she waited with bated breath for him to return. Every time he drove into her, she gasped from the sparks that traveled to her nipples and clit.

"Don't stop," she said.

"Baby, I'll give you these nice, long strokes until you come."

She could feel his heartbeat, or was it hers?

The buildup was deliberate, smoldering fire, growing

with each thrust. The sensation, the friction all gathered in the base of her stomach, waiting to usher in nirvana.

"You want it harder?" he asked, and when she nodded, he shifted them slightly before giving her faster, bolder strokes.

This was all for her. Only her. She wanted to hold off her orgasm, prolong the moment where she could pretend that Silas was hers, but his fingers found her clit.

"That's it, gorgeous. Come all over my dick," he said against her ear as her moans became unfettered.

She began to ascend, and it wasn't long before she was shouting his name while millions of twinkling stars filled her vision.

After Silas came, grunting against her neck, he simply held her and kissed her nape. When their heartbeats settled, he got up to dispose of the condom, giving her a chance to look around.

His room was bare, nothing of note except for the beautiful wooden bed frame that appeared handcrafted.

"I know I need furniture in here," he said almost self-consciously when he returned and found her surveying his space. "I just haven't figured out how to design it or what pieces to get. I don't want to overspend."

"You should go to a flea market," she said as he reset-tled beside her in bed and pulled her against his body.

"I've never gone to a flea market, but I don't think I'd like it. Too much stuff. Too many options."

"The key," she told him, "is knowing what you're looking for going in so you don't get sidetracked or over-whelmed."

"Of course you're a thrifting expert," he said, gently chuckling.

"It's fun. It feels like treasure hunting. The rejected become valued again," she said and was about to suggest she take him one of these days before remembering that would be impossible.

"You good?" he asked, pausing the scalp massage he'd been giving her. He must've sensed the shift in her mood. "You need more painkillers?"

It was the perfect time to tell him she was leaving, but she chickened out and said, "No, I think I'm ready for your carbonara."

She'd tell him tomorrow.

Chapter Twenty-Two

SILAS WOKE up to Raven in his bed, her body against his sending warmth rippling from his chest center. It felt familiar despite it only being the second time he was in this position with her.

As much as he wanted to stay in this hold all day, he needed to get ready for work. He attempted to slip out of bed without waking her, but he was unsuccessful.

"Rest. I'm just going to take a shower," he whispered.

But she sat up, pushing her braids from her face, and asked, "Can I join you?"

And minutes later, after wrapping her bandaged ankle in a plastic bag, they were under a cascade of warm water. His hands skimmed over her full breasts, waist, and ass before he lazily stroked her pussy, delivering her to the point where she orgasmed on soft gasps.

Breakfast came next, and he made her an overly involved bowl of oatmeal that tasted like apple pie. While they ate, he said, "You can stay here for the day. The left-over carbonara is in the fridge, and feel free to use the TV or internet."

"I'm going to work, though," she said.

He shook his head. "You should take it easy."

"I sit at a desk most of the day," she said with a laugh. "I'll be fine."

And her statement was firm enough that Silas clamped down on the impulse that wanted to insist she rest.

"I'll just need to stop at my place and get presentable," she said, looking down at the baggy T-shirt she was wearing.

After they had finished their meal, Silas drove Raven to her motel where she instructed him to take a seat as she got ready.

"I'll be fifteen minutes, thirty tops," she said.

But Silas could've watched her for hours flitting around her room on her crutches, grabbing clothes from the armoire and evaluating her options in the mirror by holding them in front of her body. She settled on a mid-length dress that hugged her curves.

Shortly after she disappeared into the bathroom, she called out to him, "Could you bring me that small bag next to the television?"

He made the delivery, but instead of retreating, Silas leaned against the doorframe and observed. "This how you do your makeup all the time?"

She was on top of the counter, pressed close to the large mirror over the sink. He didn't like how risky the position was, but he bit his tongue.

"No, the lighting in here sucks, and I don't have my proper mirror," she said, and while he was watching in rapt fascination as she "lined her waterline," there was a knock at the door.

"I'll get it," he said, and he found Linda Vale, the motel owner, standing on the other side.

"Hey," the woman said, her eyes widening. "I didn't

expect you here. How's Raven? I heard about the incident yesterday."

"She's—"

"Is that Linda?" Raven asked, emerging from the bathroom.

"Oh, sweetie," the older woman sympathetically said as she watched Raven limp to the door.

"It's just a sprain. I'm okay, I promise," Raven said, hugging the woman. "Silas is helping."

"Don't worry about the reception," Linda said. "I'll deal with that until you feel better."

The older woman's odd comment stuck with Silas, and when he and Raven were on their way to Mountaintop, he asked, "What did Linda mean about you not having to worry about reception?"

"I clean the foyer for a discount on my room," she replied lightly. "Every morning before work, I sweep the area, vacuum, and set up the coffee station."

Jesus, she didn't need to do all that.

"You could stay at my place, you know. I have a spare bedroom," he said casually.

Also, he had a large bed that easily fit them both.

"Thank you, but it's fine," she said with a wave of her hand, and he suddenly remembered her tenure was winding down.

She'd either be leaving Cedar or making a bid on a permanent residence. His stomach churned, but it was unclear what scenario it was in response to.

As they turned onto the unpaved road that led them straight to Mountaintop, he saw a lone car already parked next to the cabin.

"Who is that?" Raven asked, leaning forward in her seat.

"No idea," Silas said, slowing as he approached. "An eager customer, maybe?"

It wasn't unusual for people to show up early for their first class or tour of the day.

"Let me just make sure. Stay in the truck," he said as he hopped out and approached.

"Morning, sir," Silas said to the old white man who stepped out of his car wearing a shabby suit and carrying a briefcase. Definitely not here for any of the services they provided. "You need some help?"

Perhaps he was lost.

The old man stepped forward. "Yes, I'm looking for—"

"Mr. McGowan?" Raven called out from the open truck door. "What are you doing here?"

It took Silas several moments to place the familiar-sounding name. This was Chuck's lawyer.

"Ms. Coleman, good morning. I've come to speak with you and Silas Reynolds, actually," the old lawyer said. "I've made an unfortunate error."

———

Silas sat in the break room across from Raven. Mr. McGowan and his dirty glasses were at the head of the table, an assortment of papers in front of him. Silas wanted to hypothesize what the lawyer's mistake could possibly be, but to preserve his nerves, he settled on mentally preparing himself for whatever may come.

He looked over at Raven, willing her to look back, but she was focused on the old man's movements. She was worrying her bottom lip, clearly unsettled and nervous as well. Silas nearly reached over the table to grab her hand, but the lawyer spoke, bringing all attention to him.

"A few years ago, Charles made modifications to his

will," the man said. "Unfortunately, I forgot all about it and somehow misplaced the document. But it turned up yesterday."

Silas scooted forward in his seat. "You mean there's a more recent will than the one we've been following?"

"Yes," the lawyer said before removing his glasses and steepling his fingers. It looked like a practiced move. Something he did to underscore his words. "Three years ago, Charles changed the beneficiary of Mountaintop Adventures from you, Ms. Coleman, to you, Mr. Reynolds."

The air in the room went still for many seconds. And Silas couldn't draw a breath as the lawyer distributed the accurate version of the will that echoed what he'd explained. Chuck's flourished signature was at the bottom, sealing the document's authenticity.

Mountaintop belonged to Silas.

His mind was moving too fast for him to land on a specific thought until he looked over at Raven.

She was still studying the new will, her expression unreadable. But she had to be disappointed. Maybe even angry. And a knot so tangled and complex formed in Silas's stomach.

"Since no contracts or money has exchanged hands," Mr. McGowan continued, "we have survived any complications." The old lawyer was the only one who chuckled.

Once all was explained and questions were answered, Silas and Raven escorted the man to the door.

"Where can I find good breakfast in town?" he asked them.

"The Yodeling Loon is good for that," Raven said. "It's on Main Street. Hard to miss."

And with a quick thank you, the lawyer left the cabin.

"Congratulations," Raven said, turning to him with a soft smile that didn't quite reach her eyes.

"Raven—"

He was interrupted by the staff as they popped up from behind the reception desk. They all still were in their outerwear and holding their bags.

"What's going on?" Halo asked as the three quickly approached.

"We saw the car outside," Doc said. "Then we found the break room door closed."

"Silas owns Mountaintop," Raven stated bluntly. "It turns out Chuck did leave him the business."

Silas should've felt his spirit soar hearing those words again, but he did not. He was too concerned with Raven, who still had those damn sad eyes that made him want to draw her to him.

"Wait, does this mean we have two bosses now?" Bodie asked, scratching his chin.

Co-ownership.

He'd been so stuck in an all-or-nothing mentality that the idea of owning Mountaintop with Raven had never crossed Silas's mind. And it wasn't a horrible idea. He'd have to get used to it, though. Things would function sort of like they did now. He could share the burdens of operating a business with her. They could spearhead her hotel partnership plan together. It would—

"No, Silas is the sole owner," Raven said.

"So you're leaving?" Halo asked with a tinge of somberness.

The question incited a sinking feeling in Silas, and he quickly said, "Raven, can I speak to you for a second?"

"Sure," she said, and he led her back into the break room.

The words he was about to say were barely formed, but he took a breath and asked, "What do you think about co-ownership?"

"W-what?" she said, blinking rapidly.

"Co-ownership," he repeated.

Raven searched his face. "Are you asking me to stay?"

"Yes," his brain shouted, but no actual confirmation came out of Silas's open mouth.

If he thought Raven's eyes couldn't turn sadder, he was wrong because something dimmed. And he began stuttering, trying to articulate his fears, his doubts. What if she stayed and whatever connection they had turned out to be smoke and mirrors? How would that affect their working relationship? What if she never found contentment in Cedar Lake?

Raven stopped his incoherent ramblings with a smile that almost seemed like her normal one.

"Listen, you're being sweet, and I appreciate the offer," she said, "but I'm good. I've had fun, a real adventure. We both know you're meant to run this business."

"I'm sorry," Silas said softly, not sure what else to say.

"No, it's fine. This is how things were supposed to be," she said.

But if that were the case, Silas wondered why his chest hurt as if it had been trampled.

Chapter Twenty-Three

"I KNEW that massive portrait he had of himself in his office was a bad sign," Raven's mom said over video call, regarding Chuck's lawyer's fuckup.

"Mistakes happen," Raven said as she carried an armful of toiletries from the bathroom to her bed, making sure not to hit her bandaged ankle on anything.

"I was going to buy a Jacuzzi with the money I got selling Chuck's things," her mom said.

"We're lucky we didn't spend anything. I'd hate to know what the recouping process looks like," Raven replied.

It was darkly humorous how her hesitancy to leave Cedar Lake might've saved her a lot of hassle. Financially, at least.

"You seem to be taking everything very well," her mom said, but the truth was Raven was working hard to shove aside the end-of-summer-camp melancholy trying to settle.

"I had a good time, I'm leaving with a fun job experience, and I got a paycheck all summer," Raven said.

"How is everyone over there taking the news?" her mom asked.

"People are being really sweet," Raven said, thinking about the lovely remarks from the entire Mountaintop team, Linda, and a few of the locals she'd bumped into today while preparing for her departure tomorrow afternoon.

"What about Silas?" her mom asked.

Raven was hoping Silas wouldn't come up. All her feelings were at the surface, ready to burst free. "I think he's relieved," she said, careful not to reveal too much in her tone. "He loves Mountaintop. And I'm sure he's happy he doesn't have to part with his money to get it. I was an obstacle, and now that I'm leaving, it's probably going to be smooth sailing for him from here on out."

He'd offered her co-ownership, and for a split second, Raven thought he wanted her to stay. That he felt a modicum of what she felt and couldn't stand the idea of her leaving. But he'd stuttered, unable to reaffirm his offer. She realized then he'd done it because he believed he was responsible for the short end of the stick she was receiving.

"You fell for him, didn't you?" her mother said gently.

Raven didn't bother denying it and replied, "I'll get over it."

"Do you know how he feels?"

"Not the same way," Raven said, and as if suddenly too burdened by the truth, she took a seat on her bed. Her heart was too soft. She wished she were made of Teflon. Perhaps then she wouldn't have found herself in this situation.

"I'm sorry, honey," her mom said.

"It's fine. I'll be fine. I always land on my feet, remember?" Raven said with the intention to lighten the moment, but it ended up sounding a little sad.

"Love you," her mother said. "I'll see you tomorrow, and the freezer will be packed with ice cream when you get here."

It was the best news Raven had heard all day.

———

The pop of the cork on the sparkling cider sounded with accompanying heartened cheers, and Silas watched as Victor and Isaiah excitedly topped off three glasses. The kids were already in bed for the night, but the three of them stood in the kitchen celebrating Silas's win.

"Your patience paid off," Victor said, handing Silas a flute before returning to the other side of the kitchen, where he and Isaiah held each in a casual embrace.

"How does it feel?" his brother asked.

After a drink from his glass, Silas said, "It's exciting. Can't wait for what the future holds."

The husbands exchanged a look.

"What?" he asked them, shifting uncomfortably.

"You don't seem like someone who's just gotten a lucky break," Isaiah said.

"I'm still in shock, I guess," Silas replied. And who could blame him? Days ago, he'd been contemplating his next steps if Mountaintop didn't work out for him, and now his name was solely on the deed. It was enough to give a man whiplash.

"How is Raven taking all of this?" Victor asked.

"I think okay," Silas said with a shrug. "She's leaving tomorrow."

"Tomorrow?" Isaiah asked, his eyes widening. "So fast? The lawyer just showed up yesterday."

"Well, why would she stay if she doesn't have the business?" Victor asked his husband, and Silas tensed, recalling his inability to commit to co-ownership with Raven. Logically, he knew it was too much of a risk, but there was something inside him that wanted to throw caution to the wind and ask Raven to stay. The only thing holding him back was the fact that the last time he'd ignored reason, he'd gotten on an ATV and ruined his life.

Silas took another swig of his cider, wishing it had the ability to dull some of the feelings coursing through him.

He left his brother's house for his own after answering several more questions and reassuring comments about his bright future.

In his kitchen, he kept his hands and mind occupied by preparing dinner and sorting through the growing pile of neglected mail. Bills, ads, bills, archery magazine subscriptions, and more ads.

But a manila envelope stood out from the rest, and Silas paused when he saw Chuck's lawyer's name and information on the front. With no idea what it could be, Silas sliced open the envelope and removed the letter he found. He immediately recognized his former boss's slanted, loopy handwriting, and with a hammering heart, Silas took a seat at his kitchen table to read.

Silas,

If you're reading this, I'm either dead or my son of a bitch lawyer accidentally sent it to you. I really should fire that guy. You know he once billed me for taking a pen from his office? Anyway, this letter is not about my lawyer. It's about you and Mountaintop.

Mountaintop is my greatest accomplishment. I gave up a lot for it. Love, time, sleep. And sometimes I wonder if it was worth it, but then I drive up that mountain and see the cabin, and I know it was. I can't imagine a better man to take it over. Build on its legacy. I hope it makes you as happy as it makes me.

- Chuck

P.S. And if I am dead, you better not be sniffling about it. That's the circle of life, motherfucker.

Silas laughed out loud, wiping the tears that had fallen. It felt good to experience Chuck's attitude again, even if it was only in writing. His words were also reassuring.

Owning Mountaintop had been Silas's goal for a while, and he'd pour his focus into running it to the best of his ability and make Chuck proud in the process.

———

Raven had packed her bags, made sure she hadn't left anything in the drawers in her room, and was now officially checked out of the motel she'd called home for weeks.

"Visit, all right?" Linda said as the women hugged in the parking lot.

"I will, and thank you for everything," Raven said.

"Expect at least a text a week asking for crossword puzzle help."

"Of course. I'll be looking forward to them."

A vehicle's horn sounded then, and Raven turned to see Mountaintop's shuttle van pull into the motel's lot carrying Bodie, Doc, Halo, and Silas.

"You guys!" Raven shouted, laughing as they filed out one by one.

She had already said her farewells to them yesterday, so she hadn't expected them to show up in the middle of a workday. They offered hugs and more kind words that tested her resolve not to cry. Bodie told her he'd miss her. Doc assured her he'd hit her up now that he'd be in her "neck of the woods" during his fall semester at college. And Halo urged her not to be a stranger.

When she finally turned to Silas, he stood as she first saw him, imposing and beautiful. In a certain type of movie, this would be the moment he'd ask her to stay or tell her he lo—

"It was nice getting to know you," Silas said instead.

"Yeah, it was," she replied with a put-on cavalierness.

He handed her a tin box he'd been holding. "I made you some blueberry muffins for your trip."

"Oh, this is so sweet," she said, looking inside the container to avoid searching his eyes for some flicker she'd inevitably, foolishly hold on to. "Thank you."

With all her belongings in her vehicle, she looked over the assembled small group and said, "I don't believe in coincidences, so I'm glad for the mistake that allowed me to spend the summer with you."

Once in her car, Raven pulled out of her spot and gave everyone a final wave through the open window.

In another version of a certain kind of movie, this would be the moment Silas would chase after her on foot. Instead, Raven left the parking lot and merged onto the road that led her to a freeway out of Cedar Lake.

Chapter Twenty-Four

MOUNTAINTOP HAD A NEW SECRETARY, Louisa. She'd been here for an entire week, but Silas still did a double take whenever he entered the cabin and saw her behind the reception desk.

Louisa had recently moved into town with her sister after her twenty-five-year marriage ended, and her fifteen years of office experience made her a competent and efficient hire. She got along with everyone at Mountaintop, even Halo. There was nothing to complain about.

Except for the knitting.

Louisa liked to knit whenever there was a spare moment, which meant during breaks in the kitchen or when she was on a call.

It was a charming skill—hell, Silas's mother was a brilliant crocheter—but the soft clanking of Louisa's needles was getting on his nerves.

Of course, he would never express this annoyance out loud to anyone. He suspected they'd look at him like he said he wanted to euthanize the sun. And he could recognize his recent irritability was more to do with his lack of sleep than anything the nice woman was doing.

On this particular morning, before any tourists had arrived, Silas was gulping his coffee, hoping it would ease the throbbing in his head. Bodie and Halo were chatting about some reality TV show while the clicking of Louisa's needles was a steady, never-ending beat in the room.

That is, until the older woman suddenly halted her knitting and said, "I almost forgot. I found these at my desk yesterday." She pulled out three crystals from a side pocket of her purse, presenting them for the team to see. "They looked special, so I just didn't want to toss them."

Silas's heart pitched in his chest. "Raven's," he said and reached for the crystals.

Unfortunately, Bodie was quicker and snatched them up. "I'll mail them to her," he said. "She was just telling me about some new ones she'd added to her collection."

"You talk to her?" Silas asked, his voice scratchy.

"Yeah," Bodie said like it was a given.

It had been almost three weeks since Raven had left, and ever since Silas had been trudging through an unexpected transitional period of sadness. Simply put, he missed her. Which felt weird to say of someone he'd known for less than two months, but how else could Silas explain his evening ritual of scrolling through Raven's social media pages? The days she posted a picture—any picture—were spun of gold.

Silas was hopeful, however, that this compulsion and the ache that tormented his stomach whenever he thought of her would wane soon. They had to.

Thankfully, his work still brought him some satisfaction during these odd times, and today was no different. His favorite classes, as always, were his more advanced ones. When Christian showed up for his afternoon private lesson, Silas was excited to talk about his future tournaments since he'd done really well at his first two weekends ago.

"I don't know if you got my email about the upcoming competitions," Silas said to Christian as the other man stretched his triceps. "I thought you could pick one, and we could really focus on improving a specific technique."

Christian didn't immediately answer, and there was a far-off look on his face.

"You good, man?" Silas asked, snapping his fingers.

"Sorry, what did you say?" Christian said, returning to the present.

"You okay?" Silas asked. "You seem somewhere else today."

Christian hesitated, kicking the dirt under his feet before saying, "I was going to wait until after class to tell you…"

"What is it?" Silas asked.

"This is probably going to be my last class for a while," Christian said.

"What? Why?" Silas asked carefully, hoping the problem was something he could solve. Archery could be an expensive sport especially as one advanced, but there were ways to mitigate cost. If the problem was time, they could dial back on the number of lessons per month, or maybe cut the duration of sessions. And if it was—

"I'm going to be a father," Christian said, a bashful smile and red-stained cheeks transforming his face.

Silas's racing thoughts halted. "Wow! Shit. Congratulations."

"Yeah, it's a surprise. Didn't expect it," Christian said with an airy laugh. "But I want to do the right thing and financially contribute and stuff."

"No, yeah, I get it, man," Silas said and went in for a hug.

"I'm sure I'll pick it back up sooner rather than later," Christian said, grabbing his bow. "And of course you'll still be here, so..."

And as Christian found a spot at the shooting line, he was unaware that he'd already hit a mark.

Of course you'll still be here.

Why the sentiment bothered him so much, he couldn't say, but it echoed in his head like a bell tolling for the rest of the workday, on his drive home, as he made dinner, and while he scrolled through pictures of Raven.

———

"Ride's almost here," Gwen said to Raven, who was leaning against a street sign pole fighting the effects of the liquor she'd imbibed throughout the night in the building behind them.

Bass-heavy music filtered past the doors of the club and the two bouncers standing guard, but any appeal it had had hours ago was lost in the face of nausea.

"Okay, let's go. He's here," Gwen said as she looped her arm through Raven's and helped her to the Uber that had pulled up to the curb in front of them.

The backseat of the car smelled faintly of air freshener-masked vomit and sweat, but Raven no longer felt like she was bobbing across water, so she didn't care. She slumped against the seat as Gwen exchanged pleasantries with the driver.

"You're a good friend, and I love you," Raven told Gwen when the vehicle started moving through the downtown core of their city.

"I love you too, babe," Gwen said as she fixed Raven's wind-tousled hair.

Her friend wasn't the clubbing type of person. She'd have rather been at home on the couch reading, but she'd come out for Raven.

"You okay?" Gwen asked after several minutes, and Raven turned away from the hazy city lights outside her window to look at her concerned friend's face.

"I still feel really sad about Silas, and I hate it."

Raven could usually bounce back from heartbreak after a good cry session, a night out, and a week of meditation.

But she'd done all of that, and she was still discovering the depths of her hurt nearly a month after leaving Cedar Lake. It was as if she'd left a beach thinking she'd dusted off all the sand on her person, only to find more hiding in the folds of her clothes hours later.

"You made a connection, and it's not weird that you're grieving the loss of it," Gwen said.

"Sure, but I keep wondering why this time feels different than all the other times," Raven said, "and I think it's because subconsciously, sometimes consciously, I've always picked the worst guys to avoid real heartbreak."

She couldn't feel heartbroken for too long if the people she chose were awful or half-committed because she was already anticipating the end. It allowed her to prepare and ultimately brush off the hurt quickly. No lingering sand.

"So Silas is a good guy you fell for," her friend said.

"Yeah, and it scared the shit out of me," Raven said, laughing at how she'd tried to off-load the decision to leave Cedar on her intuition. She wished he sucked. Even just a little bit. Why couldn't he hate recycling or tipping or something.

"Have you thought about telling him your feelings? He might—"

"Absolutely not," Raven said, even though the hopeless romantic in her, the one who believed in the power of love, the one who dreamed and hoped for the type of affection the greats balladize about, wanted to pour her soul out to Silas.

Twenty-one-year-old Raven would've done just that, probably in a flashy outfit with an effusive speech. But the Raven of today, with more emotional bruises and lessons, knew, just like she knew the sting of rejection, she couldn't grand-gesture her way into being loved.

"It's a life lesson then," Gwen said.

Raven nodded. "I'm going to raise the bar a little bit when I start dating again, and Silas will be the prototype."

"I like that plan," her friend said.

But as Raven settled her head against Gwen's shoulder, she knew that that blissful future was a distance away because, most days, she still couldn't quite feel past her heart cracking like plaster.

———

Silas rang the doorbell to his brother's home as his niece and nephew bounced beside him with their partially eaten ice cream cones.

When Isaiah opened the door, the twins ignored their dad and rushed inside. "Thanks, Uncle Silas!" they shouted before vanishing.

"You got them ice cream," his brother said with an amused smile.

"It was on the way," Silas replied. Sometimes he picked up the twins from their dance class when their fathers were unable to.

"You want to come in?" Isaiah asked. "We got some watermelon from the garden."

"I'm good. I'm gonna head home," Silas said, moving off the stoop.

"Wait a second, I haven't talked to you in a minute," his brother said, joining Silas outside and closing the door behind him. "How're you doing? How are things?"

Silas shrugged. "Good. Nothing to complain about."

"That's good to hear," his brother responded, nodding too much and tipping Silas off to a hidden agenda.

"You're being real weird. What's going on?" Silas asked.

"Nothing… Actually, you know what? I'm going to say it," Isaiah said, throwing up his hands.

"Okay," Silas said, bracing himself.

"You said you were making lemonade from what life has dealt you, but I don't see it that way. I think you're just eating the lemon straight, rind and all," Isaiah said.

"What the fuck are you talking about?" Silas asked, truly bewildered.

"You messed up *once*, a long time ago, and now you're scared of messing up again so you play it safe," his brother said.

Silas stilled, finally clicking where this conversation was heading. "Why is it so hard to believe that I want to live in Cedar or work at Mountaintop?"

His brother laughed brashly. "Man, be real with yourself if no one else. You want to do competitive coaching. And I hoped when Raven entered the picture and started fighting for Mountaintop, you would finally admit it, but you just dug in your heels. Then I saw you falling in love with Raven, and I thought that would get you to reassess things, but instead you let her walk straight out of your life."

Isaiah stopped talking, but Silas couldn't discern the silence over the pounding of his heart. Too much had been cast at his feet at once, and he couldn't possibly begin to parse it all right then. He gave his brother a curt nod and turned to walk to his truck.

When he got home, Silas made himself a meal but then couldn't account for the actual experience of eating it. He turned on the TV and mindlessly watched until he was tired enough that sleep came almost immediately. However, his night was restless, and fatigue draped his body in the morning as he got ready for the day.

Studying himself in his bathroom mirror, he almost laughed at the miserable reflection. His skin was dull, he hadn't visited the barber in a while, and he just looked so damn unhappy.

Of course, this was the moment he thought of his brother's words from the evening before.

Mountaintop had once given him his second wind. It was the job he fell back on when competitive archery was no longer an option. It allowed him the space and time to heal physically and mentally from his injury. He owed it a lot.

But are you happy?

"No" was the resounding call from deep within. Mountaintop no longer provided solace. Because in his wildest dreams, he'd be doing high performance coaching. In his wildest dreams, he'd be traveling and seeing the world.

In his wildest dreams, he'd be with Raven.

A puzzle piece Silas had overlooked slid into place, and a sudden surge of energy had him moving urgently through his morning routine. His thoughts were similarly racing as he began constructing an audacious plan.

Executing the first part of his idea saw Silas driving to Halo's house. He had no idea how she would react, but with enthusiasm as his compass, he rang her doorbell.

When she answered, she was only partly ready for work, but he asked her, "Do you have a dollar?"

Chapter Twenty-Five

FOR HOURS SILAS drove on the highway with only asphalt, trees, and anticipation for company. Mountains flattened out and roads got busy as he entered the city. His GPS had been silent for most of the journey but was now active, leading him down roads into squeezed neighborhoods with identical, nondescript houses.

He eventually arrived at his destination, a duplex that looked as bland as everything around. But it was the address Raven had left them, so it was exactly where he wanted to be.

He was going after her with no sense if she would be happy to see him, but if anyone would appreciate a shot in the dark, a leap of faith, it was Raven.

After ringing the doorbell, he triple-checked to see if he had pit stains, and as the door opened, he took a breath, ready to see the woman who'd been consuming his thoughts. However, on the other side of the threshold stood a short man with a shiny head and glasses.

"Can I help you?" the man asked.

Silas shook his head. "Sorry, I think I have the wrong house—"

"Who is it, honey?" a woman's voice called from inside the home, and when she appeared at the door beside the short man, Silas froze mid-step.

The woman was the spitting image of his Raven, but older. Her mother?

"Wrong home," the bald man said.

"Actually," Silas said, hope rising again, "I'm looking for Raven. I'd like to speak with her."

The older woman gave him a once-over. "She's not here at the moment, but I can tell her you dropped by."

Silas felt flattened but said, "Sure, let her know Silas stopped by and that I'm—"

"Silas?" the older woman said, straightening. She gave him another full assessment. "You're Silas?"

"Yes, ma'am," he replied, shifting from one foot to the other.

"My daughter isn't expecting you. Why are you here?" she asked, her expression now steely. Tentative.

Silas thought of the different ways he could explain himself but landed on expressing the simple truth. "I'm in love with your daughter."

Raven's mom searched his face. "And you came all this way to tell her that?"

Butterflies crowded his stomach as he said, "Yes."

"Calling or texting would've been easier," she said.

"Yeah, it would have," he replied, "but I needed to see her. To tell her face-to-face."

A soft smile appeared on the woman's lips. "She's at the Casablanca flea market. She'll be there for a while."

Silas quickly returned to his truck, punched the location name into his GPS, and followed its commands for thirty-two kilometers to a congested parking area.

The market was a sea of tables, carts, and tents filled with secondhand products and quirky knickknacks. Sellers shouted for attention and customers hollered at deals, but Silas ignored everything as he searched.

He scanned the crowd, weaving in and out makeshift aisles, dodging people carrying rugs and fragile objects, sidestepping pets and strollers, and disregarding calls from vendors.

Forty minutes passed, and he started to feel certain he'd missed her. The sun had been relentless this entire time, so he was also sweating. He couldn't make a declaration of love looking like this. Maybe giving her a call or a text was the way to go. They could set up a nice meeting in an air-conditioned restaurant. But just as Silas had thought of this alternate plan, he saw her.

Raven. Her head above the rest.

She was speaking and laughing with someone, and she looked breathtaking with her big bouncy hair and bright-colored dress.

Before he could think better of it, he bellowed in the middle of the market, "Raven!"

Many people looked his way, but so did she, and when their eyes met, he felt the world make sense again.

———

"I don't know if I like the shape," Raven said to her friend as they studied a vintage bar cart.

"Yeah, the wheels make it look like a wagon," Gwen said.

The friends had been perusing the market for all its offerings for the last hour but had yet to find anything worthwhile.

They stopped at a vendor who was showcasing and

selling their paintings, and a particular rendering of the French Alps grabbed Raven. She assessed it for a moment before realizing why it had her transfixed.

"This reminds me of Cedar Lake," Raven said, mostly to herself, but Gwen approached to study the painting with her.

"It's beautiful," Gwen said.

Raven nodded, moving on to another painting. But her friend took the opening to ask, "How are you doing?"

"Good," Raven said. "I feel a little more like myself every day."

Which wasn't totally true, but she'd grown tired of being sad and exclusively listening to slow songs by Solange and Sade. Also, she couldn't bear to see her mom or Gwen look at her with pained expressions anymore. So she'd decided to fake it until she made it.

That meant concentrating on the good stuff happening in her life, like this current trip to the flea market, or the apartment she was very close to signing a lease on, or even the website design work she'd been getting from burgeoning musicians after she'd done Doc's band's website.

All things considered, she was doing quite well.

"What do you think of this?" Gwen asked, pointing at a cable spool that had been turned into a table.

"I see the vision, but this price…" Raven said, showing her friend the tag with the hefty cost.

"Oh, never mind. Let's go," Gwen said as they laughed and moved along. They were standing at another stall, when from across the way, Raven heard her name.

Someone had shouted it loudly enough to cut through the babel of the flea market, and she looked out and around the crowded area. Raven wasn't a completely unique name, so the idea that another Raven was being hailed was possible, but she felt oddly compelled to locate the source. When she locked eyes with the last person she thought she'd see today, she froze.

"What's wrong?" Gwen asked.

"You see him too, right?" Raven asked, grabbing her friend's arm.

"The giant man jogging toward us? Yeah," Gwen said. "Who is he?"

"That's Silas."

Gwen looked at her with wide eyes. "Silas, *Silas*?"

"Yes, now, what do I do?" Raven asked hurriedly.

"We can leave right now and disappear into one of the aisles."

"I made eye contact with him. I can't just run."

"Do you want to stay and talk then?" Gwen asked.

"Maybe a quick hello," Raven said, her eyes still glued to Silas, who was quickly closing the distance between them.

He was probably in the city for an archery convention, or perhaps he was picking up inventory that couldn't be delivered to Cedar Lake directly. Before she could come up with another plausible explanation, Silas was standing in front of them.

"It's good to see you again," he said, slightly out of breath.

God, he was still handsome, his voice still captivating.

"Yeah, it is," she managed after swallowing hard. "This is my friend, Gwen."

"Hi, nice to meet you," Gwen said to which Silas similarly responded, but he only offered her a cursory glance before his eyes were back on Raven.

"I think I just spotted the vendor we were trying to find earlier," Gwen said after some silence, and Raven knew her friend was giving her a way to exit the conversation.

However, she didn't immediately jump at the opportunity, so Gwen added, "I'll let you guys chat while I quickly check it out."

The moment Gwen walked away, Raven regretted not going with her.

"How is everyone?" she asked over the beating of her heart. She could—must—get through this interaction. "I saw Tess and Bodie got a puppy. Also heard you guys are looking for new tour guides. Very exciting... I didn't expect to see you here."

"It was a last-minute trip. I'm making some big life changes," he said, his eyes softening.

"Oh? Like what?" she asked before she could stop herself. Knowing more about this man would only make it harder than it already was to heal.

"Well, yesterday I sold Mountaintop to Halo for a dollar, and today I'm—"

"Wait, what do you mean you *sold* Mountaintop?" Raven asked.

He cracked a small smile. "I sold Mountaintop to pursue competitive archery coaching. It's something I've wanted to do for a long time but avoided because it was a risk I thought I'd regret."

"Whoa, that's intense and incredible," she said, her brain still spinning from the news. "So you'll get to train other Olympians."

"That's the dream," he said with another smile.

"I'm so happy for you," she said, wanting nothing more than to touch him. But how could she knowing he was planning a life she wasn't a part of? "Well, I-I should go. I—"

"Raven," Silas said, interrupting her. "It's not a coincidence that I bumped into you today. It's been twenty-eight days since you left Cedar, and for every single one of them, I have thought about you."

She was confused but trying to focus on the trajectory of his words.

"I wonder what you're doing," he continued. "If you're okay. What polish you're wearing on your nails. It's a constant running meter in the back of my head." He took a step forward, his gaze on her unwavering. "Raven, I love you."

The weight of his declaration nearly bowled her over. During the past few weeks, as she dealt with heartache, she couldn't have imagined this moment was the light waiting for her at the end of the tunnel.

"I fell for you in Cedar," she said, her heart beating wildly. "And I've been trying really, really hard to get over you."

He stilled. "Tell me you've been unsuccessful."

With a slow smile, she said, "Yeah, very."

Silas sharply exhaled and eliminated the space between them. He cupped her face like she was made of blown glass and pressed his lips to hers. It was a dazzling kiss, crisp and assuring as the first days of spring. Silas Reynolds was in love with her.

When they pulled apart, he placed his forehead against hers and said, "I'm sorry it took me so long to get to you."

"You're here now. That's all that matters," she said, wrapping her arms around him. "So what's your plan— our plan?"

"Well, I'm going to kiss you again," he said. "Then I thought we could figure out the rest later."

And that's exactly what they did.

Epilogue

Ten months later

THERE WAS a slight chill in the air, and the briny scent of the lake wafted toward Silas on a breeze.

He and Raven were back in Cedar Lake, visiting his family and the Mountaintop team for the long weekend. They'd managed to get away for a sunset picnic on the beach and now lay on their backs, staring at the stars in the inky sky.

"You're thinking about it," she said to him.

"I'm not, baby," he replied, pulling her closer to his body.

His journey to become an archery competition coach had been arduous so far—workshops, evaluations, and practicums—and he was expecting the results of a major review any day now. It had left him more than a little anxious, so Raven had suggested this outing to relax.

"I can feel your heart racing," she said as she placed her hand on his chest.

"Okay, sure, but I'm still enjoying stargazing with you," he said, tilting his head to look at her.

He couldn't totally see her under the night sky, but they'd been together for almost a year, so he'd long memorized every contour and detail of her beautiful face.

"All right, get up," she said, peeling away from him to rise to her feet.

"What're you doing?" he asked.

"We're going skinny-dipping," she said as she removed her hoodie and shirt. "It'll help you get your mind off things."

He sat up. "Raven, it's fucking cold."

She unhooked her bra and tossed it to him. "We'll keep each other warm."

"This is a public lakefront," he argued.

"Yet no one's here," she said, shimmying out of her jeans and thong. "You're not going to let me run into the lake alone, are you?"

She knew the answer.

He got up and took off his T-shirt, and Raven approached to circle her arms around him and meld their lips together. He held her tightly, embracing the buoyancy and heat she stirred with a simple kiss.

"I love you," she murmured against his mouth.

"I love you," he replied.

She pulled away after a final kiss, and Silas's pulse quickened, looking at her silhouette against the moonlit sky.

"Come on," Raven said with a laugh as she turned to run toward the gentle lake shore.

He dropped his pants and boxer briefs before sprinting to catch up to the woman of his dreams.

A NOTE TO READERS

Thank you so much for reading *Take a Hike*! I've always wanted to write a small-town romance, and I'm really happy that I got the chance to with Silas and Raven.

I hope you enjoyed their love story, and if you did, let your romance-loving friends know. Thanks again, and until next time!

Mimi <3

ALSO BY MIMI GRACE

Lovestruck Series:

Book 1: Make a Scene

Book 2: What a Match

Book 3: Take a Hike

Standalone:

Along for the Ride

ABOUT THE AUTHOR

Mimi Grace credits the romance genre for turning her into a bookworm as a teen. She now writes sexy romantic comedies in hopes they keep others reading until late at night. Besides books, she loves generous servings of mint chocolate chip ice cream, long-running reality competition TV shows, and when she spells "necessary" correctly.

www.mimigracebooks.com

www.ingramcontent.com/pod-product-compliance
Lightning Source LLC
LaVergne TN
LVHW092307191025
823828LV00009B/153